CONNECTICUT

CRITICAL ACCLAIM FOR DAVID THOMSON

'Witty, expansive, convincing, honest, more than a little mischievous and, so often, absolutely on the money. Thomson's voice is one of the most distinctive and enjoyable in film criticism. It leaps from the pages of this spruced up classic like flames from a bonfire… For as long as there are films worth writing about, Thomson's opinions will remain worth reading' – *Telegraph*

'David Thomson is a giant in the world of film criticism, and his book is the chest-crusher you might expect: erudite, delightfully tangential and surprisingly polemical' – *Times*

'Full of unexpected insights, it's learned and beautifully produced. It's also tremendous fun' – *Guardian* **(Books of the Year)**

'Chatty and authoritative… Both wonderfully informative and a beautifully written paean to the movies and their continuing ability to inspire and enthrall' – *Sunday Times*

'The greatest living writer on the movies' – *New Statesman*

'Thomson at his best (which is, bluntly, better, more intriguing, more infuriating, more fun than just about any other critic)' – *Sight & Sound*, **the BFI Magazine**

'Rigorous and rewarding, and a page rarely passes without insight' – *Independent* **(Books of the Year)**

ALSO BY DAVID THOMSON

Movie Man

A Bowl of Eggs

Hungry as Hunters

Wild Excursions: The Life and Fiction of Laurence Sterne

A Biographical Dictionary of Film

Scott's Men

America in the Dark: Hollywood and the Gift of Unreality

Overexposures: A Crisis in American Filmmaking

Suspects

Warren Beatty and Desert Eyes

Silver Light

Showman: The Life of David O. Selznick

Rosebud: The Story of Orson Welles

Beneath Mulholland: Thoughts on Hollywood and Its Ghosts

The Alien Quartet: A Bloomsbury Movie Guide

In Nevada: The Land, The People, God, and Chance

Hollywood: A Celebration

Marlon Brando

The Whole Equation: A History of Hollywood

Nicole Kidman

'Have You Seen…?': A Personal Introduction to 1,000 Films

Try to Tell the Story

The Moment of Psycho: How Alfred Hitchcock Taught America to Love Murder

The Big Screen: The Story of the Movies and What They Did to Us

Moments That Made the Movies

Why Acting Matters

How to Watch a Movie

Breaking Bad: The Official Book

Television: A Biography

Sleeping With Strangers: How the Movies Shaped Desire

A Light in the Dark: A History of Film Directors

Disaster Mon Amour

CONNECTICUT

DAVID
THOMSON

kamera
BOOKS

First published in 2023 by Kamera Books,
an imprint of Oldcastle Books Ltd,
Harpenden, UK
www.kamerabooks.com

© David Thomson, 2023

A CIP catalogue record for this book is available from the British Library.

ISBN
978-0-85730-564-0 (Paperback)
978-0-85730-565-7 (eBook)

2 4 6 8 10 9 7 5 3 1

Typeset in 11.25 on 14.25pt Minion Pro
by Avocet Typeset, Bideford, Devon, EX39 2BP
Printed and bound in the UK by
CPI Group (UK) Ltd, Croydon CR0 4YY

'We cannot erase the perplexity that comes from assuming our mental health practitioners are sane – just because that is their aim in life. Don't a patient and a doctor need something in common? And doesn't the patient dictate the rules and rhythms of this game? Under some guise of being unwell, he or she tells a story. So doesn't the doctor need to be a little disturbed, just to keep up?'

Dr Frederick Kinbote, private conversation

'Accordingly, we should regard the midsummer's eve in the Connecticut forest not as the preparation for a wedding ceremony but as an allegory of the wedding night, or a dream of that night.'

Stanley Cavell, 'Leopards in Connecticut',
Pursuits of Happiness (1981)

for Douglas McGrath

A Note from the Publisher

Our author, your author, has never lived in Connecticut – but there are so many places he has not lived, and that shortcoming has not deterred him. (We can't be everywhere – we couldn't even feel that possibility until the movies came along.)

But our man is resigned to living in his head, and suspects that most people are familiar with that zip code. The head can create many locations that have enough external 'reality or atmosphere': a job, family life, a place, common interests, being American, industrious wickedness, tragedy, whatever. You know those dreamy aspirations and the generous ways existence plays along with them.

Our author's residence was more truly the movie screen. And that's how he has lived in Connecticut – in films like Bringing Up Baby, The Lady Eve, Sullivan's Travels, My Man Godfrey... *the list goes on.*

Connecticut was often an idealized setting for retreat in films of a certain era (just before the War – which one? you ask!), an Arden or an al fresco canvas where people who made books, theatre and movies (and money) often liked to go, to 'a weekend place in the country', where they could relax, run a little wild, and think up their next projects as if they were sane and businesslike 'successes'.

Think of Connecticut as the hoped-for countryside in an age when the city was beginning to be a collection of solitudes, crammed together, like a prison. The rural state was a place for ease and abandonment, for screwball comedy, and wondering if you were in love. That is my Connecticut, and I like it in black and white.

It is where the actress Margaret Sullavan chose to live when she fell out of love with the movies, yet not quite aware how being there could endanger her precious yet precarious marriage to Leland Hayward. It was in Connecticut, on 1 January 1960, in a hotel in New Haven, that she was discovered dead.

We'll come to that, alas.

PART I

ONE

There I was, busily writing my book about the kiss in cinema – I had a deadline – when these two strangers walked right in and told me I had to go to Connecticut.

'Why? Why there?' I said. Haven't you felt the dread of being abruptly taken away?

My lithe young research assistant from the Dominican Republic, a danseuse, so alert, trembled – as if perhaps she had inadequate papers – at this intrusion. Then she simply slipped away: I've never seen her since. Let me tell you, researchers like that don't grow on trees.

The only thing that happened in the face of my protest was that the two strangers in gray and grey, my 'they', gave me the civilized runaround. I felt like a ball bouncing off walls, unable to avoid the thrash of their rackets.

'Oh, it's lovely in Connecticut,' rhapsodized number one. 'This time of year: summer, with cuckoos in the distance.' Who expects such feelings from uninvited strangers?

'I would go to camp there as a lad,' added number two. 'Happy days. Blue nights. The pals we had then. Marshmallows? I believe we had marshmallows. Doesn't one toast them over a camp fire?'

'Connecticut's days away,' I told them. No one does geography any more. I like to read maps, as if they were books. But the point about Connecticut, it seemed to me then, was its rural remoteness, a sense of never needing to go there, while entertaining idle thoughts of it as an innocent retreat. If one ever felt a need to escape.

'Its distance is its charm,' explained number one.

'So the closer one gets,' I interposed, 'the less charming it becomes?'

'Don't be so lawyerly,' said number one. 'It's not what one expects from a learned fellow with your credentials, writing an entire book about the movie kiss.'

'Connecticut has a gentle, pleasing shore,' number two advised. He could have been quoting. 'With many sylvan prospects in the interior.'

'Fuck Connecticut,' I said, just to be clear about my position.

'You can't.' One smiled at two. 'That can't be done.' He seemed rather smug about this.

'No physical dignity in it, much less satisfaction,' said his friend. Have you caught their rhythm by now? The way they took turns. Their lines might have been scripted for them.

'You'll feel calmer there. It's known for being salubrious, soothing and –'

'Very quickly you'll feel better,' the other interrupted.

'Better?' I pounced on that. 'Who – may I ask? – has decided that I need to be better?'

'Look,' – this was number two – 'it's where people like you go. In the nicest way, old sport. There are as many clinics there as wayside inns. Be grateful for small mercies.'

Number one chimed in: 'It's all a matter of safety.'

'Safety?' I asked. 'Whose safety?'

'Yours, old chap.'

'What do you mean people like me?' I said. All this old chap, old sport, smokescreen: it was getting me down.

There was throat-clearing between one and two and then they explained it to me.

You may have known this, but I had never heard it before (and

I do think it has been kept suspiciously quiet): Connecticut, the entire enterprise, all 5,567 square miles, the Nutmeg State, Branchville and Darien, New Haven and Hartford, Brookfield and Hazardville, Windsor Locks and Crystal Lake, Sandy Hook and Southbury (you can look them up – you'll need a map), its varieties of landscape, town and country, the condition, the state, the idea, was a mental hospital, or reservation, the way Yucca Mountain in Nevada once upon a time was where we were going to put all our horrible, shit-faced nuclear waste. Those were the days. If only we could have them back.

'But I'm writing a book,' I insisted.

'Nearly everyone in Connecticut is,' said number one reassuringly.

'It helps to pass the time,' number two concurred. 'And I hear it can have some therapeutic benefit, over the long haul.'

'You said "quickly",' I pointed out. 'Quickly I'll feel better. You did say that.'

He sighed. He rolled his eyes at the notorious volatility of 'creative' people. 'There you go again,' he said.

'You're really too suspicious.'

'Paranoid.'

'Not well.'

'Nuts.'

'Loopy.'

'Off the deep end.'

'Screwball.'

* * *

It wasn't my doing. They told me to think of myself as someone in a story, but that was not helpful. I couldn't tell whether I was meant to be a character or an author. It didn't matter what I said. They had a grammatical inversion ready for making any defense seem like self-incrimination. I protested that I was in the middle of a sentence when they had knocked on my door, and number one just shrugged a shoulder and said, 'Most of us are, most of the time.'

Did he mean the life sentence? That is one way of looking at things. I nearly wrote a movie once, about a fellow living what seemed like an ordinary, humdrum life, until bit by bit clues appeared to suggest he was actually in some kind of institution, an asylum or a kindergarten. An intriguing set-up, maybe, but I never knew how to end it. If you have any ideas…

Here is the odd thing. I'm warning you. No matter how wronged you are, you can begin to think you *do* need to go to Connecticut. Is there a fundamental shame just waiting to be identified?

'So what are you thinking now?' asked one.

'Yes, I thought I saw some secret thought,' said two.

There was an air of mocking hide-and-seek in their interplay. I felt I was hiding in a doll house with huge faces gazing at me through its tiny windows. It felt slightly lewd.

'I really don't remember,' I said, and folded my arms like a determined child. 'After all, I think of many things.'

'Oh, my word, isn't he a marvel?' said one. 'Too many things, I daresay.'

'Loss of short-term memory is common in your condition,' said two. 'It's just one more bit of proof. I'll make a note of that.'

'I wouldn't be surprised,' said one, 'if you don't even remember our names.'

'You never told me!' This made me furious. 'You never *said* your names. Come to think of it, you offered not a jot of identification or authority.' I wondered if that omission might still keep me out of Connecticut.

'Of course, we told you,' cooed number one. 'Let me say, old bean, in the friendliest way possible, you may be a little farther gone than you realize.'

Two chipped in: 'As for our authority, I hope one glance is sufficient. We're hired for that, you know. One and two. I mean to say, no one ever asked John Wayne about his authority, did they? Do I mean John Wayne?'

'Of course, you do,' said number one. 'No one ever doubted the Duke. His authority was as plain as the nose on your face.'

One took a couple of steps sideways, as if to reappraise *my* nose – and I can tell you that I have never had a discouraging word about that part of me. Indeed, several ladies have noted how tidily it fits during the act of kissing – which, as you know, is a professional matter with me.

'You never uttered one word about your names!' I insisted. I was getting scared and angry, and often in those moods I need to laugh out loud or have other people laugh at a joke. 'You're just the party of the first part and the party… of the eleventh part,' I added. Eleven, I find, is often comical. I don't know why.

'No,' said one, shaking his weary head sadly. 'We are better placed as numbers. You'll learn to live with it, if you're patient.'

'Why mention patients?' I asked.

'Why, indeed?' despaired one. 'Instead, let's think of you as our companion on the journey.'

'That sounds agreeable,' said two. 'You'll have the back seat of the car to yourself. You can stretch out, if you want to. Let it be a vacation. The leather there is like chamois, and there are magazines in the pockets behind the front seats. Are you a golfer?'

'*I am not*,' I said. I tried to make golf sound like an unnatural or unAmerican activity.

'Pity,' said one, 'I seem to remember some golf magazines in the flap. But I think there's the usual departmental porn, too. More to your taste, kisser?'

'I abhor pornography,' I told them. You have to make some things clear as soon as you can.

'You'll get over that in Connecticut,' said one – really, I found it more comfortable to think of them as numbers. 'Connecticut is vigorously against abhorrence, you know. Its liberalism is a byword, and that will bring enlightenment in your treatment. All the latest research – whatever. You're a lucky fellow. You do realize, before Connecticut things were on the primitive side, brainbox-wise, if you know what I mean.'

I didn't know what to say, but like most of us I harbored grim pictures of how the allegedly insane passed decades and decay in state hospitals for the some-such. I could hear the groans, the screams, the announcements of drab routine, and the bored mirth of the guards. In my head I had been there. You too?

'Connecticut can go to hell,' I decided to say.

'So be it,' said two in an easy-going way, 'but let's get you there first. And don't be taken aback, old boy, if it turns out heaven.'

'Anyway,' I remembered. 'Show me your identification. Just exactly what are you two? To whom do you report?'

'To whom?' echoed one, and two chuckled in an amiable way. Sometimes laughter can chill your marrow.

'What are we?' said two. 'We're company for each other – what does it look like? And we're here to take you to Connecticut.'

'Do you have a requisition order?' I demanded. 'Do you have a note or a chit? Some paperwork?'

One looked at me in a pitying way. He shook his head and seemed tired, or was it just nostalgia, a memory of the time when authority had meant something? 'No, we don't have a chit, not even a billet-doux. But we have you. Come along, kisser, like a good boy. You don't want us to summon up a touch of the nasties. Do you?'

I didn't say anything. Not yet.

* * *

I awoke slowly in the back of the flowing car. My waking and its motion merged, like fluids in suspension. That restful coming back from wherever – sleep, the night, anxiety – hadn't happened to me for years, so I tried to make a gradual act of self-composure. Usually in those days I woke up suddenly as if a gun had slammed or a door been fired. So it was pleasant to see a passing canopy of foliage and trees watching over me. I felt I was being looked after, on an early summer afternoon. Isn't that what we're hoping for? I yawned, I stretched, I was at ease, even if the heads, one and two, were still there, like placards in the front seats.

On that afternoon, my dreaming tended in opposite directions: a part of me was kissing Grace Kelly (or was it Sandra Dee?); another wondered if I could feel a tumor growing in my head. Sometimes it can be best not to puzzle over one's own mind.

'Good nap?' suggested one. He did not look back at me, but I saw kind eyes like gray pigeon breasts in the rear-view mirror.

'Must have been,' I realized. I was still having to appreciate what had happened. 'Yes, a satisfying sleep, quite a good one. I feel I got some rest. Reminds me of Sussex.'

'Ah, Sussex!' sighed one. 'Did you ever know Eartham Woods?'

That name struck a chord. 'I did once,' I told him. 'Yes I did.' (But this was no time for heartbreak – you see, I had my own life, kept it to myself. I was very far from just *their* character.)

Two said, 'We're going to stop for a leak and a sandwich. Interested?'

'I never eat leeks,' I said. 'They don't agree with me.'

Two laughed in a good-natured way. He turned and looked at me. 'Not the vegetable,' he explained. 'A pee.'

'Yet a pea *is* a vegetable, isn't it?' said one, and the three of us chuckled together. It was an escape from our tension. Who can keep that up? I can but I suppose that does seem hostile.

'A pee might be handy,' I said. Might be very welcome. Like all ordeals, stress has its consequences. I suppose on the trains, to Auschwitz or wherever, people relieved themselves in their clothes, as they stood. (No, I'm not going to cut that just because it's upsetting. What's a story without some dismay?)

The car pulled off on the side of the road with softened bumps and the squeak of grass against the tires. We were in the heart of a forest, not dense to the point of impenetrability; there were glades and clearings, natural resting places and what looked like promising picnic spots. But there was not another person in sight. It was what you like to expect of the depths of the countryside, in the forest. I could see birds spinning lazily between the treetops on thermals of warm air.

There were ferns beneath the trees that came up to our waists, and that thick brewery aroma of growth cooking humidly in June and July from ground so soft it might be flesh. I guessed there could be rains here, thunderstorms, or temper fits in the weather. The ferns had the span of an eagle's wings, with every arrowed frond flawless, every serration immaculate and shivering. I had not encountered nature in so long, or so luminous in the shade from the trees.

There I was, there I had been, attempting to compose a provocative gift book on kissing in the movies (it was that or car crashes), recasting every sentence, laboring, striving, organizing, and suddenly I was in a part of the forest, one small aspect of it all, without any other observers except for one and two, and the profusion of unimpeded growth. There was no anxiety, even if an owl and a fox had rhyming eyes of knowingness at what might come.

'It is lovely,' I agreed. The word came out like a sigh. I heard myself say it.

The three of us walked into the woods and each found a tree to pee against. The glossy ferns bounced and swayed as I touched them. I saw two chipmunks watching me, as if no humans had been there before.

I could see the distance through the trees. There was the fissure of a path, or some kind of passage, to get away, like the vein in a leaf.

'You could escape perhaps,' murmured one, beside me, surveying the way into the woods. 'You're younger than us – if you can run.'

'I was a promising half-miler once,' I admitted, amazed at my impulsiveness. '1 minute 53 seconds, personal best,' I said and I felt my muscles tighten.

'Really?' said two. He seemed impressed, as if thinking of past masters, Lovelock, Whitfield, Snell, and Wottle, half-miling smilers. 'Not much point, though,' he added.

'Oh, why not?' I wanted to know.

'We've been in Connecticut a couple of hours,' said one. 'You were asleep when we crossed the state line.'

'*This* is Connecticut?' I cried. Had it happened just like that, without any sign of border patrol, confinement, stockade, detention camp or customs? Indeed, this place felt airy and open, balmy and fragrant, it –

'We did tell you how pretty it was,' said one.

'I could still escape,' I said. I reckoned that if I took that faint path it would lead me on, running, running.

One was zipping up. 'No,' he said, 'you don't understand yet. You see, you're *here* now. You're *in* the state. Wherever you run to, it's Connecticut. You can no more escape than you can stop being an Aquarius, or left-handed.'

'I was never left-handed,' I said, but I was stung that they knew about Aquarius.

'I mean if you were. Have a sandwich?'

They had a brown paper bag. Two opened it up, miming surprise. 'Take your pick,' he said. 'We've got a BLT, a ham and Swiss, and a roast beef, with all the trimmings, but no onion – I hope you won't miss that. We detest the smell of onion in the car. What do you fancy?'

It felt like a trap or a trick question in one of those party games where you can be found out. Ham and Swiss was my favorite, but why should I tell them that, my warders? My hijackers, even if it was such a fine day in Connecticut and they were being so affable. You have to stay on your guard.

'You pick first,' I suggested. It was ordinary civility.

One and two looked at each other, hummed a little tune I didn't quite recognize (it was on the tip of my tongue), did as I asked, and handed me the ham and Swiss. It was limp and warm in Saran wrap. But it was a hefty beast, a meal, and I could see the bread had seeds and oats in it.

'That all right?' asked one.

'I won't complain,' I said.

'We could swap,' offered two.

'Not unless you prefer to,' I countered.

'It's for you to say,' said two.

'You're quite sure?' asked one, and his tone of voice seemed to insinuate that certainty could be a rash move in the game. Whereupon, a friendly male voice called out from the forest. There he was, strolling towards us with light behind him, without explanation, but an ideal figure to illuminate and define the wilderness. He was epic, but casual, and quite endearing. It was a tall, untidy fellow, coming out of the forest, and he was saying in a cracked baritone, 'Gee whiz, any chance you fellows have another of those sandwiches? I've got a hunger on me, I can tell you.'

To be exact, he said this twice; he had to repeat the line and his entrance, having flubbed the first attempt when he seemed to say, 'I've got a hanger on me, I –'. A hushed voice from somewhere said, 'Let's go again.' So, obediently, and without complaint, he turned around and came strolling out of the trees, take two, as fresh as a breeze, as if for the very first time. And now the line was right – without so much as a clapper-board to mark it. He was a natural, momentary and authentic. There could have been a statue of him there in the glade, bronze, smiling in the sun, careless of destiny or debt, 'The Rambler'.

This fellow gave every appearance of the classic hobo, a bum, a tramp, a gentleman of the road. He wore a battered fedora, a faded white shirt threadbare at the collar, a jacket with one pocket hanging loose. His corduroy pants were so worn I thought I could see the white of his legs. He had on what seemed to have been alligator shoes once, but they had split open so that his bared toes might have been the alligator's teeth.

Best of all, in terms of expectations, he had a stick over his shoulder, a length of ash, and a full swag bag tied to its end, red with white polka dots and bravely cheerful, even if it let one surmise that a man's life and possessions, his past and his memories, might amount to no more than the size of one oven-ready turkey.

'Hi, gents,' he said, and he had a smile for the three of us. 'You can call me Sully. Two weeks ago I escaped from a chain gang. How about that?'

His head, his hands and his throat were all tanned, like furniture, not when polish or wax have been applied, but from weathering and the abrasion of use. It was not a darkness gathered on a two-week walk, or even from months on that chain gang. Deeper down it was good old Californian suntan. He might have been a lifeguard on Santa Monica beach, waiting for kids to splash and cry out in the surf, and he had the shoulders of a swimmer.

'I didn't realize we had chain gangs still,' said one, breaking his sandwich in half and giving a piece to Sully. We all did the same, so Sully found himself the owner of a small feast.

'You bet they do,' he said. 'Down south of here a way.'

'Where was that?' asked two.

'You know, they never said,' Sully explained. 'But it could have been Georgia, maybe, or Alabamy.'

'You've come a long way,' I observed. The sandwiches were good and they enhanced our new comradeship.

'Riding the rails,' said Sully. 'You can wake up in a different world and weather. Where you guys headed?'

'We're going to Dr Bone's place,' said number one. 'The Retreat. It's not far now. Fine establishment, feels like a country club and it works wonders.'

'Sounds swell. Think I could ride along?' asked Sully.

Whereupon, one and two looked at me, as if it should be *my* decision. That was unexpected, but I didn't feel inclined to argue, not when I liked this wanderer. 'Why not?' I said.

'Well, that's bright of you,' said Sully. 'That's decent, I gotta say. It'd be pretty nice to have someone to talk to. Walking in the woods is fine, especially these woods here. Good woods, they are, the real thing. But you can get to wondering if you're ever going to meet a soul again. And if you do, whether you'll still know words and manage to utter them. I mean, a fellow can be walking along and talking to himself, the way you do as a kid if you're carrying a message. Remember that sort of thing? Why, once I had to keep it in my head, a message from my father to my mother, for more than a couple of miles, that he wouldn't be home that night. And he wasn't – not ever again. Last I saw of him. That's how I was feeling – darned lonesome – coming through these woods and just not knowing where I was but –'

'Oh, enough, please,' said number one in a weary way. Somebody had to stop Sully. A bronze Rambler is all very well, but a speech of more than four sentences pushes your luck.

By the way: I don't think I quite took this in, but when one and two put me in their car – back in the city – it had seemed a stylish but modern limousine. But now, in the woods, in a very well-kept way, it felt somehow older, a classic if not quite an antique. As I say, I did not fully appreciate this at the time. But it was so long since I had been in a vehicle that had the space, the calm, the soft engine hum, and the cool leather of a civilization.

* * *

In the car and on our way again, Sully and I were together on the back seat. It occurred to me in the confines of the car, despite the perfuming of its interior, that my new pal from the open road might have a vagrant aroma – unlaundered clothes, failure to find a decent barber, a rough diet, and even the habit of taking a dump in the undergrowth, that sort of thing. Yet, closer to Sully than I had ever been, all I could detect was what I thought was Old Spice, and recently applied. The more I looked at him the more I began to wonder if his nutty sheen and his outlaw air of being beyond the reach of social services were something of an act. His teeth were outstanding and bright from a recent whitening that did not fit my sparse knowledge of life on rural chain gangs. But common sense doesn't always do as it's told, so I was a little suspicious of Sully my new comrade and chance acquaintance. Who knows these days if it's life in the raw, untrammeled, disorganized, at random, one has wandered into, or –

'Used to go everywhere in these limos,' said Sully. 'Something you get used to, I won't lie to you.'

He had stowed his stick and swag bag and he was examining the furnishing of the limo.

'There should be a handy cocktail cabinet around here,' he mused, searching in the gloom. 'Fancy a stinger? I used to make a good martini, set you up, so bracing it was just as if someone told you your fiancée was dead this morning. Ever had a fiancée die on you?'

'Never,' I insisted. I had no idea who was listening, or what was being recorded.

'Funny feeling that,' said Sully. 'Breaks your heart one minute, then the next it gives you fresh hope. I made a picture once about a fellow on his honeymoon. This lovely new wife he has. But already before lunch he's wondering if he's bored. Open-minded. Second day, he's on the beach, fetching a praline daiquiri for his bride, when he meets another woman and knows right off he has to marry *her*.'

I was perplexed. 'So this just married fellow divorces his new wife and marries another?' Could that be an automatic process?

Sully was nodding enthusiastically. 'Picture was a hit. A lot of folks, on their wedding day, you know, they're thinking of someone else. Is that a hoot? Surveys say so. Motion picture polls.'

So I hadn't been crazy! I thought I had detected the assurance of a Paramount in Sully, an air of unhindered romance from the silver screen and the energy for following any crazy story under the sun. 'You are a movie director!' I was delighted for him, for both of us.

'*Was* is the word,' said Sully. 'I was a wow, too. *Hey, Hey in the Hayloft, Ants in Your Pants of 1939* – did you catch those?' He strode on through my ignorance. 'I had hits like apples. Then I was the chump. Decided I was tired of silly comedies and I was going to take to the road, see the nation, get acquainted with hard times – that sort of stuff. The studio thought I was bananas. And they were right. Where did my travels lead me? – to the chain gang, that's where.'

'But couldn't you still recover?' I wondered, full of the romance of movie ups and downs. 'If you went back now, think of the story you'd have to tell. A classic comeback!' I wanted to encourage him. I wanted to see that movie, or be *in* it.

'Well, I appreciate that,' said Sully. 'And I take it as a mark of friendship, but the powers that be, from Universal to Metro, they have a fixed idea now that I'm crazy. Why do you think I'm here, hiking through Connecticut? No second acts, buddy, no second chances. Ben Hecht told me once, never go to the bathroom at a party, and never give the audience an interval.'

If friendship was being proposed (despite the delicacy or uncertainty of our situation) I thought I would plunge in and establish myself. 'As a matter of fact,' I told Sully, 'I am at present writing a book on the kiss in the movies.'

'You are?' His eyes lit up and he turned to examine me more closely. I suppose he had been taking me for granted. 'A whole book? That's a hell of a thing. Friend of mine invented a kiss-proof lipstick.'

'How did that work?'

'I never knew. I guess, you could kiss all day long and the rose carmine never smeared. You were just as perfect as when you started.'

'Yet I like the look of red staining the mouth,' I told him.

'Well, sure, in life, I guess.' He spoke of that domain as if it was a foreign country cut off by quarantine restrictions. 'This was for the movies. I mean, if you've got Fonda and Stanwyck only until six o'clock, a smear-proof lipstick can save you time on make-up.'

'Did you ever direct those two?'

'*Positively the Same Dame*, it was called. Stanny was a peach to work with but Fonda could be a pill. Still, that worked out on this picture. Her character had to tease his a lot, but I never told him it was a joke. So he got more uncomfortable while she was giving him a boner and he couldn't stop it. Of course, we were in close-up, mostly, so you didn't see the boner. But those two knew about it, believe me.'

'*Positively the Same Dame*?' I repeated. I thought I knew them all. 'That must have been some time ago?'

Sully made ruminative shapes with his face, as if being on his own in the forest had left inroads on his memory. Yet maybe life was easier without it? Still, he made an effort at guessing, '1940? Maybe '41?'

I didn't know what to say – how could he regard 1940 as just 'yesterday'? – so I tried, 'Happy days. They don't do a lot of that stuff now,' I explained to him.

'That so?' he said, and there was no grief or resentment. 'That mood's gone?'

'I fear so,' I said. 'Though some people still fall in love with Stanny on the screen,' I reassured him. Enormous studies were being written on that slim minx. 'You still see her look and hear the voice.'

'That's nice,' he said. 'That falling in love thing, it never stops, even if you give up everything else. When it comes to it, we're just accident-prone idiots, that's what I say. Always ready to fall. Know the feeling? You can feel you're not safe going out. Think I might take a snooze.'

'Why not?'

'To tell you the truth, I'm afraid of not waking up again.'

'I'll rouse you,' I promised, and Sully laid a hand of friendship on mine. His was as brown as turned earth and mine was white, like a shoot hoping to find the light.

* * *

Editor: Let me make quite sure I'm catching the drift here.

Agent: By all means.

Editor: So, our author…?

Agent: Yes?

Editor: It's him, our man, Thompson –

Agent: Thomson, actually.

Editor: Of course, the film fellow, Biographical… whatever?

Agent: The very one.

Editor: But he's a character here, so to speak, this rather nervous fellow –

Agent: Doing a book on the kiss in movies.

Editor: Yes! That's a tempting subject actually – with the right illustrations?

Agent: We should discuss that?

Editor: We could, but first he's doing this story where he's shipped off to Connecticut, when that state – the whole shebang, am I right? – is a lunatic asylum.

Agent: So to speak. But rather more a reservation, a place of gentle assignment. There's nothing unduly punitive about it.

Editor: Aha, but can the inmates leave if they want to?

Agent: They are not encouraged to want to. They are regarded as residents.

Editor: He's made this up – the Connecticut thing?

Agent: I'll leave you to wonder.

Editor: Amusing idea. I've known a few people there, not a million miles from that. I've been to house parties there like emotional obstacle courses.

Agent: Haven't we all? Very much a weekend place for eccentrics.

Editor: And they all like to act as if it's paradise.

Agent: Isn't that the American attitude?

Editor: And is there also a hint that our man has been carried back into the past?

Agent: Into the heyday of the screwball era. Those lively years of Depression and exuberance.

Editor: So the people he's going to meet there, some of them, will be characters from those movies? We'll get to Cary Grant and Katharine Hepburn? I love those two.

Agent: Plus Carole Lombard and William Powell. That's the plan.

Editor: Will readers know the movies?

Agent: The story will speak for itself. But we can have some help at the back of the book – a key, if you like. We can say that Sully is Joel McCrea in Sullivan's Travels... *or based on him.*

Editor: First class. What an enticing scheme. So where are we going next?

Agent: To the Retreat, one of the most distinguished psychiatric clinics in the state.

Editor: Aha, I see – I think I see. But this Retreat place is going to be a little strange, right?

Agent: It is an enterprise dedicated to rest and healing – there are often mishaps in that plan.

Editor: Sadly so.

Agent: It's in a looking glass, if you know what I mean.

Editor: I do.

Agent: Farce with a touch of disturbance.

Editor: Exactly. You know, I feel quietly elated about this.

Agent: Moi aussi, mon capitaine.

* * *

No one dared break the silence at the Retreat board meeting. The several appointed members sat in a mix of helplessness and tension. Did this quiet mean there were too many conflicting ideas waiting to be put forward? Or had these fortnightly progress chats led the participants to face the *impossibility* of progress? This unuttered dismay left the minutes so incoherent that the secretary, Miss Alice Swallow, had broken her pencil point (again) trying to keep accurate notes.

'You're pressing too hard, dear,' Dr David Bone had advised her, and she had blushed furiously as she held up the splintered end of her sturdy HB, until he had murmured, 'Never mind, Alice. Not to fret.' While being aware how fretting was this poor woman's destiny.

Bone could not forget the turmoil from years ago when Alice, his administrator then as well as his fiancée, had told him they were too busy to get married, let alone explore its physical ramifications. Organizing his schedule, she had shelved their nuptials. And now in her long-buried bitterness there was one more crushed pencil.

'Can the Retreat really not afford an effective sharpener?' complained Miss Swallow, striving to maintain a positive attitude. She knew her Dr David Bone was pledged to calm and would ignore upheaval in its cause.

It all came back, how minus the honeymoon, and what with David being swept away by the disruptive arrival of Susan, the marriage with Alice had gone by the books. Yet Alice had persevered in spirit and Bone guessed she still nursed blind hopes of an eventual union, like winning the lottery. Most people wanted to be married or in love, the doctor knew, and so many chumps expected to win the lottery. That only drew more gamblers into the contest, making the odds against winning heavier still. And while they were all waiting to win what were they going to do except rob banks, do crosswords, or go off their rocker?

Treating losers in life's lottery was a designated business of The Retreat and Dr David Bone ran the show as well as he could, granted that his snappy way of speaking could turn case histories into anecdotage while barely masking his sketchy book knowledge of psychology and psychiatry. He had been trained originally as a paleontologist – what was 'Bone' meant to indicate? – until a clerical error had put him in charge of The Retreat itself. But as his colleague, Dr Fritz Lehman, had explained it, 'There are jewels hiding in every mistake, Bone. Your work with skeletons trained you in scientific structure and methodology. If anyone asks you what two and two make, you don't have to think twice. Add the white coat, plus your very engaging manner, your knack for dropping cheeky wisecracks, and you may be as good as we'll ever get.'

'Fritz, you're a tonic,' decided Bone. 'So what is the mistake in *your* curriculum vitae?'

'I'd rather not say,' Lehman blushed, 'but it's buried in my hobbies.'

'Actually, I do wear a fresh white coat every day of the week,' Bone told him. 'Susan orders them by the gross from Haverhill.'

In truth, Susan (his consort, his angel, and his fierce director) would not let David be seen in the same coat more than a single day. 'The white fades,' she declared. 'And it's the brightness that gives patients hope.'

Whereupon the double doors to the Retreat conference room opened. This signaled the approach of the Chairman of the Board himself, Horace Pike. He was a beer tycoon, an ale alumnus. He had a sweet nature despite his deep bass voice and its steady note of foreboding. He had laughed the first time David Bone had quipped that Pike's enormity was not simply attributable to his consumption of beer – it was the barrels themselves he must have devoured.

Still, there was no truth to the stories that Pike had once – in the Yale-Harvard game of '22 – crushed a young running back to death (a member of his own team!). That fellow, tackled in short sight, actually lived seven more years, albeit in a wheelchair with a breathing machine, all paid for by the Pike Fund (along with a supply of favored melodies, Shakespeare plays and Wodehouse stories on recorded disks). And all this without a trace of self-promotion for Horace himself. (It was enough that two out of three Mrs Pikes had called him 'crusher'.)

'Well, ladies and gents all,' growled Horace Pike, settling into the chairman's chair – it had been made for him by blind craftsmen in Lyme. 'We'd better make a start if we're expecting lunch.' He had an agenda before him, just a page, but his perplexed look made it clear that he did not believe it was sufficient to deal with what he called 'the pickle' they were in.

'Seems to me,' he said, 'it's time to draw some lines in the sand.'

'If we can see the whites of the lines,' said Dr David Bone.

'Or tell the sand from the gravel,' added Dr Fritz Lehman.

'Well, let's just skip that metaphor,' said Susan with her customary briskness.

'For God's sake!' Pike implored. 'Can we move on with business?'

'Item 1 is "Definition",' said Miss Swallow. 'It still is. We have never settled that.'

'So we've been in business eleven years without knowing what we're doing,' cackled Susan, who seldom let a Swallow remark pass without a shot – and Susan could shoot, putt and fence with the best modern pentathletes. 'What a lark! Aren't we managing OK? Why fuss over "Definition"? That could stop us in our tracks.'

'Right,' agreed David, 'we're a work in progress. As long as we keep progressing, no one can get a fix on us. Don't you see?'

'But there are the numbers!' roared Pike. 'It's not just regular transit, like one and two bringing in Kisser here, and Sullivan the other day. That had paperwork you could read. It's what Connecticut is meant to be all about. "Bring us your sick and afflicted." Am I right, Kisser?'

I nodded (yes, it was me), in the way newcomers are ready to be part of a consensus. You see, I had been instantly appointed to the Retreat Board as its Patient Representative, before discovering that other inmates, more experienced or soured, had given up on governance as a folly. I was laboring under the hope that to appear businesslike and willing might seem like signs of my getting better and being released!

'Aren't we a teacher's pet?' murmured Susan, without looking at me, but blowing smoke-rings into the room. I leaned towards her, and whispered, 'I daresay your husband would prefer you not to smoke. Research says it corrodes the brain.'

'My what?'

'Your hubbie,' I said, nodding towards Dr David Bone.

She laughed out loud, and it was loud, as if she might be a little deaf or somewhat on edge. 'You silly dope. We're not actually married.'

'I thought,' I began.

'No, no, no,' chattered Susan. 'We're not married because we are determined to avoid the risk of divorce. It's divorce that is undoing the fabric of the country.'

'But we do have five children,' said David with a wry grin, enough to imply that in the way of fabrication he might be contemplating more.

'Well, we behave like bunnies, don't we?' admitted Susan. 'We'd be zombies if we didn't have that. It's as old as suffrage and hygiene.'

'Now, there you are,' said Dr Lehman. 'I think that illustrates our dilemma perfectly. What is expected in rabbits – a doe can have 400 offspring in a lifetime – would seem inappropriate in humans. I use the word "inappropriate", you understand, in quotes as a convenience.'

'Talk for yourself!' said Susan. 'This is the old abstinence taboo rearing its tired head. Womankind, and unkind, have been faced with that so many times. Self-denial is a primary cause of derangement – I believe that's clear. Let's expel the taboos.'

'Taboo or not taboo,' said David Bone. Not his best; not his worst.

I thought I had something useful to contribute, a chance to speak up. 'Don't you believe the word "bunny", as in bunny girl, to describe a waitress or entertainer who conveys looseness or promiscuity is a case in point?'

Susan stared at me as if I had walked backwards through a bramble bush. 'My good man, what *are* you talking about?'

'The bunny girl, *Playboy*,' I said, 'that entire operation.'

'What in heaven is play boy?' Susan demanded. 'And bunny girl?'

Could Connecticut be so sheltered? 'I thought everyone knew about that,' I began. 'Why, it must be fifty years old by now.'

'When did this happen?' asked Susan.

'Oh, the 1960s,' I surmised.

Susan burst out in a riot of laughter that had a note of hostility or panic. When some people laugh, you can smell danger in the air. 'Well, it's perfectly obvious why you're here,' she said. 'Regarding the future as history!'

There was general confusion, raised eyebrows and the repressed anxiety that feels disorder coming, like a tsunami or a tremor in the ground. Anyway, I was informed by Chairman Pike's kindly assurance (he had a diary in his pocket, the size of a hotel bible) that this was only 1941 when madness was not yet a tradition but a wayward breeze in sensible society.

* * *

Eureka, California. On the Sunday after Thanksgiving, 25 November 2012, a family of three were walking their dog on the wide open beach in conditions of strong wind and a surf that was sometimes as high as ten feet. The sixteen-year-old son threw a stick into the water and their dog went in after it. When it seemed that the dog was being carried out to sea, the son entered the water to attempt rescue. Whereupon, as the son appeared in distress, his parents went in after him. The boy regained the shore but by then the father was out of sight. So the boy and his mother re-entered the ocean in search of the father. Nothing more is certain. The father was drowned, and the mother. Both bodies were washed up on the shore. But the boy is still missing. The dog survived.

* * *

This unfortunate episode did occur, though some of the participants may have had different accounts of it had they survived. Don't overlook the irony that the one speechless creature left was barking and helpless. But don't count on irony as a protection. Our grim show is past that now.

Be wary of deciding waves have what might be called a mind of their own. Still, if you grant that waves had fallen on that shore (just north of Eureka) for let's say 10,000 years (I'm being hypothetical and conservative here)... are you with me? Watching waves can fill a life. And we calculate that with full tidal ebb and flow there might be 3.1 million waves in just a year, one after the other. And that is times 10,000? I had to look this up (you might, too), but the answer is... look, work it out yourself. But you and I know that the waves had beaten there so much longer than 10,000 years.

Does this give you a headache, just to think of so much unobserved energy?

Anyway, the Eureka misadventure had currency for a time: a detached sympathy was mixed in with wistful admissions that it was a funny old world, make no mistake about that, as well as 'you never really know'. People encountered the incident with degrees of wonder or being wounded. It was as if readers were oddly charmed by newspaper stories of distant mischance.

This was on the northern shores of California where, in all likelihood, you have never been. But I will tell you that that coast is magnificent: there are hundreds of miles of hard, white sand formed by the waves. Over so many centuries those waves have beaten the land pale. So, if you can picture Eureka, take it for granted that some disconsolate youth in Connecticut might have read this item about the family and their dog just three weeks later and taken it as a tipping point (you know that theory?).

I wasn't there – no one was, for the youth's mother was out – but I can believe that this lad didn't know whether to laugh or cry, that he took fresh pains to ensure that black masking tape shut out the light from his windows, and that he counted, cleaned, and treasured the collection of weapons that his mother kept in the house ('at least a dozen', it would be said). We can call him Adam Lanza, if you like. An unlikely name, you say? Does it leave you imagining this twenty-year-old strolling through his own empty house miming to a record of the booming Mario with 'Be My Love!'?

TWO

I saw her standing there in Connecticut.

Keep it as simple as that. A single shot, full figure. We have become used to closing our eyes and having a magical spectacle, like a gift, or a life, before us.

I can't help it; I have no better way of saying it; I see dreams in daylight. I tottered out of that addled board meeting and there was Irene standing in the gardens of The Retreat like primavera.

A man can see a woman standing before him, and be so moved he wonders if he is being transformed. Do you know what I mean? Do you remember that daze? If you don't, perhaps you should stop right here, put this book down and go back to staring at your wall. I say this without any wish to offend, but there may be less hope for you than you need. You have your wall and so try to make it a screen.

Do you feel uncomfortable if I address you directly? You want me to stay as discreet as that blank wall? Are you planning to offer a defense that *you don't quite exist*, that you are only there like the ghosts in a cinema, watching it all but unseen by the bright figures in the picture? Just how deranged are you?

Forgive me: you don't have to answer that, or make the attempt. I know such matters are beyond mere privacy, they are in the unlit interior, the inwardness, where any hope for reason keeps bumping into the possibility that we are unsound. Try to see the funny side of it.

Whatever... I saw her standing there, a slender blonde in a green silk dress like a sculptor's wet cloth draped on a warm clay work in progress. There was a regal look on her face that forbade any mundane comment: why shouldn't she be standing there in the garden in broad daylight in a dress so deco, so *her* that it was fit for the best Manhattan scavenger party in the depth of the Depression, 1936 or 1937?

Of course, she was 'beautiful', whatever that means; in this case the woman herself – Miss Irene Bullock – was an implacable believer in her own beauty – so long as her scenes could be shot quickly before time started its erosions. Have you ever known a beauty whose serenity was not subject to panic attacks at the idea of aging or half an hour waiting – as if it was a wasp in her hair?

Irene was standing on a lawn, the green of which was intimidated by the jungle hue of her dress. Her cigarette had a carved ivory holder. She seemed like sophistication, yet she noticed me when I was hardly fit for her class. I was a fresh inmate in Connecticut, unfairly ripped from my kissing assignment, none too sure of myself or my mental health. I heard birds singing – don't ask me which ones.

'Are you a forgotten man?' she called out to me. Her voice had a curious hollowness, or was it utter confidence?

'I could be,' I said, on the spur of the moment. It did seem like reasonable casting – after all, who knew me now, apart from that vanished Dominican dancer, and the several Connecticut folk?

'Well,' she decided, 'come along with me. We have to hurry, please – as usual I'm late.'

The one flaw in her self-assurance was this jittery habit of being pushed for time.

So she glided across the lawn to meet me. I say 'glided' for she moved without friction, like a camera on tracks. This was more easily accomplished because she wore no shoes. Her feet were pleasing, the toes like marble. And by concentrating on them I was spared the test of not staring at her nipples, ditto dots, so apparent beneath the vapor of emerald silk.

'Where should we go?' I asked.

'Oh,' she said, flummoxed, but resolute. 'I never know. What a dunce one becomes in Connecticut. A few weeks here and you wait to be told your every entrance and exit. Do you know what time it is?'

'You have an engagement?' I asked.

'I think so,' she said. 'I do feel late.'

'What makes you so restless?'

She gazed at me as if the question had not occurred to her before. You can't decide to be hungry or in need.

'I desire everyone I look at,' she said. I felt that I, my person, had so little to do with this. 'I can't wait to see if people like me,' she said. 'I want to do it straightaway. Come.'

Whereupon, she reached out a designing hand – I saw there was no watch on her wrist – took my arm and drew me to the ground. How do we know what's coming? Has our spirit been there before?

The grass was dry and sweet and the ground was soft enough for us. I saw daisies close to my eyes and ants on blades of grass like seamen in a ship's rigging. Soft enough for what, you ask. Well, I trust it's clear what happened, then and there, very swiftly, and I don't think I am the person to go into the detail. How could I be sufficiently objective? After all, these things manage to be always different yet always the same. As you know already, kissing was more my subject.

I did think this as I was falling into the wrestling of tongues. In their urge to be uppermost or in support, as they slide together like double s's, they are eels swimming in a Sargasso of salivas.

She was less dedicated to kissing than I was. But when she saw my addiction, she did her best – deep down in her, I could detect a digestive fragrance, not exactly floral, but as fresh as the blossom on trees and promising kindness and calm for bees. Then soon enough she was finding other positions and energies so that it was my turn to be obliging. I hope I wasn't a disappointment. You never know, but she lapsed into a half-hour of sleep there on the grass, using her green dress (and my shoulder) as a pillow. I was in some cramped distress, but I said nothing until slowly she woke and freed my arm. Her body was milk and steel in the sunlight.

She looked at me. 'Were we in love then?' she asked. 'You don't happen to know the time, do you?'

'I think we may have been.' I didn't want to be difficult or fussy about it.

She said, 'I'm Irene, how do you do?'

We shook hands, two naked hands, with hers as cool as mine was warm. She had a silver bracelet with sapphires; it seemed like a relic of handcuffs. But no watch, still no watch. You really should imagine some of these details for yourself. (Don't just sit there like the past.) But I can say that Irene used her dress daintily to soak up the moist efflorescence on her china thighs.

'You *are* an animal,' she murmured in a detached way, and I was glad to be. She put the dress back on and the silk was creased and darkly stained. There was a tear below one armpit. I felt unexpectedly good about that. Why? I wonder: for the dress would likely be thrown away. I guessed Irene Bullock did not bother with cleaning or repairs.

'Why are you consigned to Connecticut?' I asked her.

'Nymphomania is what my card says. Maladie d'amour.'

'Sounds like music,' I suggested,

Irene smiled. 'It's the mania à la mode. Every man is looking out for it.' She saw my anxious gaze, and that cold hand caressed my cheek. 'But not you, my sheik. Not you. Do you think it's half past yet?'

* * *

I would like a cutaway here, please, a cut to some ordinary Connecticut home. This is not a complicated shoot. It won't need sound or a full crew – I could shoot it myself. All it requires is young Lanza with dull and staring eyes, alone in his house, looking at the family weapons and wondering what to do with them. No more than that. Five or six seconds on screen, enough for the idea to settle in.

* * *

Irene said I should accompany her to a party, despite my warning that parties and I did not get on. I told her she had probably had the best of me there on the lawn, but she looked somewhere between askance and aghast, as if to wonder, had that really been my best?

Did I nurse a domestic dream of settling down somewhere in fondness and improving conversations? Sancerre and sincerity. Never mind, that was my own disturbance, the battle between solitude and longing that had qualified me for Connecticut. Irene was unimpeded coition, but like a bee always sniffing another bloom up the road. Being alert to love's gratification made her a stranger to loyalty or persistence.

She advised me on the way to the party. 'Don't bother with the love business, will you? We can do thingy whenever you like, you only have to make an appointment, but none of that Valentine's Day fuss.'

'I'm not sure I can do it if I'm not in love,' I told her.

'You still do love?' She looked at me, as if I had an unfortunate speech impediment or a harelip.

'For instance,' I said, and I was bashful about this, 'I love the mere thought of Margaret Sullavan.'

A surge of attention stopped her in her tracks, a kind of bliss. 'Snap!' she said. 'I often think of myself as a role Sullavan might play.'

'But she never has sex on screen,' I pointed out.

'Only place she didn't,' murmured Irene, with a rather curt edge. 'Lord! You sweet lost boys. Come along, now, we're going to be late.'

Not that there was a sense of timetable or punctuality. The party was simply occurring in a listless way, succumbing to the warm day like five past four or new blooms wilting in the sun.

The gathering was in a sunken part of the garden, a crazy-paved area hedged in by abundant rose bushes, so planted that the blooms shifted yard by yard from unblemished white through ivory, cream, butter, custard, peach, apricot, amber, vermilion and so on through all the shades of red going from a faded pink to a carnal blush and scarlets that burned the eye.

Tables marked the corners of the suntrap courtyard and on their lacy white cloths were the drinks and canapés of a smart get-together.

'What's this party for?' I asked Irene.

'Nothing I can think of. Just another party. You can meet my family.'

'They are *all* here, in Connecticut?' I marveled.

'We were assigned as a group. Most mad families gang together. While sanies go their solitary ways.'

I was trying to remember whether that observation was Tolstoy, RD Laing or one of the Kardashians when, like a loaded truck, Alexander Bullock came in sight, the fingers of one hand beringed with snacks, the other clutching a flute of champagne.

'There you are!' Bullock cried out to his daughter Irene. 'In a pretty party dress, too. You see, darling, all you need for a party is a room and the right people.'

'I don't call this a room, Papa,' said Irene. 'This is just a Connecticut garden, cluttered up with our woeful family and people we can't remember.'

'Don't talk about your mother that way,' said Bullock. He glanced across the open space to where his wife, Angelica, was wondering whether to believe the tasteless flattery being poured over her by Carlo, so clearly a gigolo it was a wonder he had been allowed into the country, let alone into Connecticut.

But Mrs Bullock called out to them, 'Have you heard what Carlo just said?' Her voice fluttered over every word, a mad bird hoping to alight on a lost syllable.

'What did Carlo say, mother?' asked Irene, as if it was expected of her as a line she had uttered at more parties than there were rose bushes in sight.

'What?' asked Angelica. 'Carlo, what *did* you say?'

And Carlo replied, 'My dear lady, I can't be expected to remember everything I say.'

'Or anything,' muttered Bullock. But then he stirred himself at the arrival of a silver-haired ramrod who held a replenishing tray of brimming champagne glasses. This butleresque fellow wore tails, with a white bow-tie. 'Godfrey,' cried Bullock, 'It's so infernally hot here, do you have an Allagash ale, pale and cold?'

'I expect I can manage something, sir,' said the manservant, turning on a dime or a dance step so that the champagnes on his tray shivered in unison, like a line of chorines making a pretty hip-hitch.

Godfrey was back swiftly with a tankard of the required ale. Bullock grasped it with both hands and moved to slake his thirst. He seemed energized by it, so next he said, 'Ice cream, perhaps,' sniffing the air, before heading off in search of salted caramel.

'Mr Bullock appears flustered,' I said to Godfrey. The gentleman's gentleman looked at me, assessing how far he could go, and murmured, 'His chief stress is family, sir. The Bullocks are not restful company.'

'How long have you been in service with them?' I asked.

'"Service" is not the word. Just four years, yet it feels like an eternity.'

'Why not submit your notice?'

He raised a gloved hand in despair. 'I have done so, sir, many times. It is ignored. We *are* in Connecticut.'

'But why should *you* be here?' I knew I was prey to inappropriate remarks and unpredictable actions, but I did not see how this polished Godfrey could ever seem unbalanced or missing a screw.

'My own fault. Irene found me – I surmise she has found you, too, from the stunned look in your eye. I was a resident of the city dump at the time, at the southern tip of Manhattan. Just an ordinary failure, an educated has-been, you might say, but doing no harm. I had agreeable company, cigar butts to last the year, and half-full bottles of claret tossed out from passing yachts. Then Irene came by on a scavenger hunt, looking for what she called "a forgotten man", some outcast. She picked me, and for my sins I agreed to be chosen. Then, in the car driving to the Upper East Side, in traffic near the Pierre, she ravished me – I expect you know how that works. Worse yet, I fell in love with her. Your impeccable manservant is also a chump. So I found myself installed chez Bullock as the butler.'

It did seem possible. Doesn't everyone feel a need to be rescued, and wasn't Godfrey officer material?

'Of course,' he pushed on, 'the family were unmanageable. They wanted to be "eccentric". They kept horses in the living rooms. It drove me closer to desperation. But I spoke in sentences, and that can charm the rich. Irene insisted on me being her beau, her butler beau. She feared I might be attracted to her sister, Cornelia. You have not met her? Irene hates Cornelia and that rivalry made her desperate to keep me as her servant. She cannot see that Cornelia hates Cornelia, too, as much as she loathes Irene. I yielded. Irene has limitless physical needs.'

I judged that Godfrey was close to fifty, but he was as trim as a rapier or a Dorothy Parker punchline. I remarked on this to him, and on how appealingly proper he seemed.

I could see him giving judicious consideration to what to say.

'Servants are a last promise of order, sir. We guard against something going wrong, a failure of timing or table setting, the asparagus overcooked, the beds not warmed, a missing cufflink – any sin against order. Have you read Jeeves, sir? Those first books felt like Socrates on the Somme. But who will serve the servants?'

'Have you thought of medication,' I suggested.

His eyes narrowed, as if the topic was outside his time period. 'I call that Scotch,' he said.

'Drugs,' I said. 'Tranquillizers, benzodiazepines. At rest, at peace,' – I know this litany by heart now – 'all things in their place, all voices low and calm.'

'It sounds like a polite funeral,' said Godfrey. 'That's the risk in too much order. It smells of death and decorum.'

I laughed out loud. 'But if you're a manservant, a butler, isn't it crazy to be suspicious of good order?'

He gazed at the roses, the tables, the guests, the party, the day, the weather, and he nodded as if appreciating a clever trick that hardly worked now. It may have seemed like a photograph from the *Illustrated London News*, circa 1914.

'Did you dream of marrying Irene?' I asked. 'Should you let yourself live here as a servant?'

Godfrey wavered. 'I did think of Irene once as a mate – that turned out checkmate. Then Cornelia waits for her sister's discards, just to bathe them in her wondrous regret. I've loved them both, and at the same time. That's their game – watch out for it. But our servant class won't last long. If we get into this war – and I think we're bound to –'

I was about to interrupt, but I held my silence. These days it's hard to keep up with wars and I had no idea which one he meant that I might not have heard of yet. Sarawak? Guinea-Bissau? Kazakhstan? Still, there was something in his tone and the idea of 'getting into' a conflict that had me anxious.

'If we have to fight Hitler and Tojo, that won't be any picnic,' said Godfrey, though he seemed experienced with picnics. 'Count on it, most of the servant class will be chopped down – as they were in Flanders. That's how war destroys society. The country will be impoverished, so the toffs – the people who had butlers, chambermaids and gardeners, once – they'll be broke and shamefaced and it'll be impossible to get good help.'

All I said was, 'Ah, *that* war.' He was too knowing or confident – albeit on the gloomy side – for me to spell out what would happen. And what happened, if you think about it, was worse than Godfrey could have imagined.

Since August 1914 and its failed attempt to warn the Archduke, haven't we lived with the prospect of an imminent and very complete war?

* * *

Editor: This hero of ours? Our narrator.

Agent: The leaf in the wind?

Editor: Do you think he should have a name? You see, I want readers to like him. To be on his side, the wind in his sails. Imagine him fighting his way out of the Retreat, out of this wacky Connecticut – getting his life together. With Irene perhaps as a girlfriend? I know, she's on the wanton side, but they've made a start, haven't they? Actually, my own wife – my present wife – was under care when I first met her and still has her shaky weekends. Anyway, I do think a name could make our man more likeable.

Agent: *You don't like 'Kisser'?*

Editor: *Is it a touch disrespectful?*

Agent: *I could speak to him about it. But I'm not hopeful. And I don't know that Irene should be viewed as a reliable pal.*

Editor: *No? Well, at least she's a sexpot in good clothes. That's a start. And Kisser – if that's what we have to call him – he does seem stronger in Connecticut than when one and two collected him.*

Agent: *The country air has been good for him.*

Editor: *Funny you should say that – I don't think I've told you, but I have a little place myself, just a cottage, past Fenwick. Does me the world of good to get away there. I just set the damn manuscripts aside and listen to Ravel – the string quartets. The F major.*

Agent: *Fenwick? I knew a woman once who lived there. I believe she had a leopard.*

Editor: *Really? A pet?*

Agent: *No, neither one of them was what I would call tame. Does your wife listen to music?*

Editor: *She prefers to stay quiet in the city. She rests.*

* * *

I had wandered away from the party until I could no longer hear the music of laughter or glasses kissed in toasts. I feared that after half an hour in a crowd I might begin to feel rattled. I become sad or angry unless I can get away – the sort of morose shadow no one appreciates at a party.

The elegant garden tapered off into the untended beauty for which Connecticut is admired. I crossed a meadow with butterflies as company, pretty notes on a stave, and then I entered the dappled shade of a stand of beech trees. I looked up at their reach, their foliage, their color and lovers' initials carved in their thin bark.

Beyond the trees was a soft slope that led to a valley hinged on a ribbon of river, glossy in the sun. I could see no one, but a woman's cries were drifting up from the distance. They seemed grasped by another sound, of coarse male laughter, rude and aggressive. All at once, the peace of Connecticut felt undermined.

The wailing I heard was soon explained. There was a dip in the slope off to my left, sheltered by a few oak trees. In that clearing I saw two women slumped against a tree like sacks of corn with men standing over them, hunters guarding their quarry.

These two men were uncouth and hostile. They could have been numbers eleven and twelve, with small whips. They were using them to beat at the women, though on that warm afternoon they had wearied of the sport. Then I realized that one of the women was Mrs Angelica Bullock, Irene's mother. Endeavoring to protect her from the lashes was a younger woman, dark-haired and astonishing – because it could have been Irene in a wig. I knew this must be her sister, Cornelia. She was being beaten herself, but her beauty had a deeper fatalism, a mark of some ingrained injury or acceptance.

This young woman seemed to register what I saw in her. She called out, 'Excuse me, sir, won't you help us, please? I am Cornelia Bullock of Park Avenue.'

Mrs Bullock was crying piteously, as if she had gone over the edge where any recovery could be expected. The sight of her was distressing, but it was a curiosity, too. Disaster can take your breath away; its most shocking aspect is in sustaining our interest. So I spoke up in my inept way.

'I say, you fellows,' I cried out, 'stop that immediately. It is horrid and inhuman.'

Call him eleven: he looked at me and sneered. 'Au contraire, kisser, it's all too human. There are parts of Connecticut you should realize where punishment is the preferred form of discourse.'

'Ridiculous,' I declared. 'Everyone knows now that Connecticut is a haven for troubled spirits.'

I hoped this was so, though I had not forgotten that even my one and two had had a germ of that menace associated with secret policemen in their manners. I *had* been taken to Connecticut under orders, and while life there seemed – so far – a mix of whimsicality and startling opportunity, I could imagine those two turning ugly enough to flay a couple of respectable bystanders. It can be a short step from nurses to guards, from one and two to a hundred and eleven or twelve. Things get out of hand.

My thoughts might have gone further, but at that moment, no more than a football field away, there was an explosion. There was no warning, not so much as a screaming across the sky as something came down on us. My first guess was that disruption had occurred in the ground itself, like an impatient mine. There was a rain of earth and small stones, clods of grass and the aroma of gunpowder. The shock stopped Mrs Bullock weeping and wailing. Her agonized face grew still, or passive, seeming to sense jazzed-up molecules in the fragmented air.

'A bomb?' whispered eleven. 'A doodlebug? You never know when they're coming.'

'Dirty pool,' agreed twelve.

Their alarm soon made them forget me and the Bullock ladies. The two men went up to the smoldering crater left by the explosion, searching the skies for another when it was clear that whatever it was – missile or thunderbolt – had come unheard, unseen, but instant and devastating. Pinned in that vulnerability, they ran off into the trees, their suits looking like prison garb.

Cornelia Bullock gazed up at me – there were raw streaks from the lash on her throat, and her Mainbocher suit (it was the famous Wallis Simpson blue) was torn in several places. Her dark hair was wild, but appealingly so. Her mother was huddled in her arms, her system astonished by how the blast had sucked up breathing for a moment. I felt Cornelia surveying me, speculating on my capacities or story value.

'We had a block on Park once,' she said, absent-mindedly,' you'd never know it now, with a gymnasium, a pool, a matching pair of Bonnards, parrots, horses and stables, our own beauty parlor, personal trainers, and doormen who were like family. Life was pleasant, and wealth meant not having our follies noticed.'

I tried to tell her this was a history of the twentieth century. In addition, I suppose I was in love again; this was as tiring a habit as Irene's need to couple with everyone. And Cornelia had her own air of impossible desirability like a song you never get out of your head. So I told her, 'One day soon we'll be listening to Ravel.'

With her mother in her lap, tattered and torn the two of them, Cornelia laughed like broken glass falling. 'You hopeless fool,' she said, as if nothing would change her mind.

There was a suave gloom about her like the hush of elocution and death sentence. 'I was lost in that madhouse on Park since the age of eight. So I decided my only chance of controlling my madness, was to *pretend* to be daft –'

She had it all worked out as an end game. 'Night after night after chaos in the house, I went to bed counting time – Irene wanted me to do that, she has a phobia – I would say four-five-six-eight (she never noticed seven was gone!). She'd have a tantrum. Just to stay calm I imagined I was advising the president on making everything better.'

It was unnerving, to hear this persuasive account of lucidity assessing its own defeat.

'This is what crazy me did,' she said. 'I saw the risk of going mad. I thought of doing something terrible to my sister. I set the household clocks wrong, and stole her wristwatches. I worked it out like a play, with Irene going frantic about being late. But she did all her stuff out of instinct. She wasn't acting. She was a natural. Sometimes the servants gave us a round of applause. Sweet people. I wonder where they are now?'

'By the way,' I whispered, 'excuse me, but I believe your mother is dead.' I thought I should say something.

'I know.' She agreed; she consented to it. 'It happened several moments ago. The shock was too much for her.'

'So we are alone together,' I told her. Cornelia looked at me as if I might be a stray dog come home. She smiled, and I wondered whether that was just a tremor of politeness. How do we trust what characters mean or why they smile? Some people have killed their mothers first – four head shots, the body peaceful still in bed, in pajamas – in case they forgot that task in all the later excitement.

THREE

After we had buried Cornelia's mother (without adequate tools it was not the quickest task – people are not trained in burial now), she and I wandered in Connecticut in mourning and early evening.

'That *was* your mother,' I said – I wondered if it wasn't a time for lamentation or reminiscence.

'Don't go on about it,' she asked. I could not tell whether she was being brave or simply indifferent.

'To be candid,' she said, 'I think I feel free.' Candor can kill talk sometimes. I looked up at the sky, darker now, but flawless, an imprint of the heat in the lapsing day. Skies must learn to ignore so much.

'She was a silly creature,' Cornelia tried to explain. I wondered if that had left the daughter harsh or humorless.

'Why do you keep studying the sky?' she asked.

'I was looking for the seam. Or a join.' I found it hard to think of the sky as unbroken, unrepaired, a single thing, whatever.

'You're the cracked one,' she said, but that seemed to comfort her.

'I didn't see a lot of sky where I'm from. The city.' I told her bits and pieces of the circumstances I had had, the writing. I did mention the dancer and her moves.

She shuddered. 'How sordid,' she said, but I felt she was a little more appreciative.

We had no map, but there were few obstacles in the natural

spread of the land. I wasn't sure if I had escaped from the Retreat or not; there was something all-encompassing in that countryside. We camped under the stars and in the moonlight of the state without knowing where we were. We were companions, singing our separate silent songs. 'Moonlight in Vermont' is a natural song title borne on the rhythm of its words – 'telegraph cables, they sing down the highway'. But no one ever thought to write 'Moonlight in Connecticut'. The word 'Connecticut' seems like a barrier to rhythm. Yet Connecticut in the moonlight can be a treat – twilight on the Housatonic! Was stillness ever more eloquent?

And there had been that drastic, unexplained explosion. Those things don't just fade away. They can return any time you start to relax.

So I thought I should think of some subject for conversation if Cornelia Bullock was not going to decide I was a dullard.

'Do you enjoy the comedies of remarriage?' I asked her.

We had nothing else to do, no food to eat, just Connecticut and the moonlight. When she shivered, I had offered her my jacket, but she said it would have clashed with her wrecked blue Mainbocher. I thought that was being churlish. But why complain? Really, one could scream sometimes – life can be so much easier being alone. At least if I had been with Irene we would have had sexual intercourse every hour or so – what is that but a way of denying solitude?

'Comedies of remarriage?' She glanced sideways, as if she believed my head was affected by exposure. She had no idea what I was talking about, or did the juxtaposition of comedy and marriage put her nerves on edge?

I tried to be helpful. 'I mean pictures like *His Girl Friday*,' I labored. '*The Awful Truth, My Favorite Wife, The Philadelphia Story*, and several others, in which a couple much in love get a divorce for some reason or –'

She interrupted me. 'Don't skate over those precious reasons, maestro. She has a fling with someone at the tennis club. They spend more money than they possess. He's out of a job, or more interested in the job than in life at home. Then the money dries up.'

'Are there tennis clubs still?' I asked.

'Of course, there are, with lawyers as umpires waiting on the divorces. Why do you think "love" is in the scoring?'

That was definitely an item. 'Fifteen-love' after a drop shot of exquisite spite. A service that humiliates your slowness – 'thirty-love'. And then a volley to scorch your eyebrows – 'forty-love'. So much hostility with love being tolled like evensong.

'Have you ever been remarried?' she wanted to know.

'Not even married.'

'I thought not. The idea of marrying the same person twice – it's certifiable. Murder would be more sensible.'

'Why do you think of murder?'

'There's violence in our air, don't you think? I don't much trust this tranquil Connecticut that seems to go on forever.'

Cornelia and I might have starved, wandering in that state. Of course, every almanac declares Connecticut is a farmland state, fertile and provided for, arable as well as dairy. There are tidy fields laid out like squares in a quilt. At times, the state seemed benign, but it had a deeper indifference, too, a way of trusting nothing but nature and time. It didn't seem to need people. Was that how someone had the idea of depositing all the crazies there?

We had been driven to scrumping raw potatoes in the fields and drinking cold stream water in which there were acidic strands of green and purple, enough to make us wonder if the busy industries of the state might be dispersing their toxins.

Cornelia was staring into its depth. The stream had become a river. Enchanted music swelled up. I was ready to put a restraining hand on her arm, but very quietly she said, 'Do you suppose we could have a dip?' She was gazing at the river bitterly.

'Why not?' I asked.

Then she stared at me in a disapproving way. 'You want to see me naked.'

I wondered. 'I won't look if that upsets you.'

'Then I needn't do it,' she told me.

'Why would you wear a Mainbocher suit,' I wondered, 'unless wanting to make people imagine you without it?'

'Are you imaginative? Do you picture me skinny dipping? In a pond, in a heatwave, in a minute. You poor dreamer.'

We did drink from the river, no matter the suspect hues. I should also say that even in its wilder parts Connecticut was not a wilderness. The Huron and the Iroquois may have fought there once, but two hundred years of cultivation, photography and property taxes had left the landscape trained. So a path could be made without a machete or a bulldozer, or without abusing wilderness.

Without our noticing, a tall handsome man appeared in the river. He was walking in the water but he wore plaid swimming trunks and his bronzed body shone with moisture.

'Fancy meeting you two,' he said. 'Aren't you the Warmerdams?'

'Not at all,' said Cornelia, put out at the claim of some social connection.

'So sorry,' said the man. 'Thought I remembered you from a party at the Welds – two summers ago? Time runs on. You can't keep hold of it.'

He thrust out his hand – a strong grip – and said his name was Ned. Could we guess what he was doing? What an adventure he was on?

'How could we?' asked Cornelia, with an instinct that this man might be dangerous. He did seem strong.

'I got this idea,' he said – he had a blazing smile – 'to swim home across the state – well, our part of it. How do you like that? So many pools, the occasional lake, a river, this nice stream.'

Cornelia had no sympathy. 'Why would you do that? Don't you have a car?'

The man considered her question. 'I know,' he agreed. 'You can say it's folly, but I had a few drinks and got the idea in my head. Sort of like a fable,' he suggested. 'It seems a touch Arthurian.'

'Are you from the Retreat, too?' she asked him.

'Lord no, I'm not the retreating sort. Not Ned Merrill.'

'Where are you going on your strange swim?' I asked. I was touched by his confidence, or was it simply damaged courage? What other kind is there?

'Oh, I'm headed home,' he said, as if the answer was obvious. 'I'll be there for dinner – my wife, the girls. Just like usual.'

'How far is that?'

Ned stood up and tried to calculate the wooded ridges like sleep in the distance. 'Four miles maybe. Hard to tell in this light.'

'Better aim at breakfast,' snarled Cornelia.

He wasn't put out. He had this lovely, patient grin and perfect teeth – they shone in the dusk. 'That's fine. I'm a breakfast man.' He seemed the sort of fellow anyone would like, but Cornelia was suspicious of flamboyant hope.

'With a double vodka,' she sneered.

Ned chuckled, but he did take me aside, out of earshot. 'This one you've got here,' he said.

'Yes?'

'I were you I'd take her in the bushes and give her a thorough talking to. Teach her a bit of politeness.'

'You would?' I wondered.

'If I didn't reek of chlorine I'd do it myself.' There *was* a chemical, sneezy atmosphere about him, the trace of all the topaz pools he had swum through.

'I admire your journey,' I told him.

He looked at me, full of fellowship. 'Yeah? Me too. I think I do.'

He smacked me on the shoulder and then he was gone, leaving his friendly grin hanging in the air.

You want to say this sort of asiding makes *Connecticut* the book, our book, harder to read. But, I beg you to consider that Connecticut – like other states – is not just a site for tidy, arranged meetings, but a screen or a sky on which so many stories have played. Ned Merrill was far-fetched, I daresay, but I can't forget him, and I never look at a pool in the distance, azure in the greenery, without being reminded of his pilgrimage.

'Who are you talking to now?' asked Cornelia.

'It doesn't matter,' I said shamefaced. 'To them I suppose.'

She looked past my shoulder at where spectators or readers might be (think of them as you), without a tremor of belief at first, and yet… I studied her disapproving loveliness closely and I think she had a twinge that there might be something like an audience or onlookers in the dark, or in the twilight of our private forest.

She asked me, 'You know talking to yourself can be a sign of schizophrenia?'

'It can be safer than talking to others,' I said.

She did smile at that, not at me, or my attempt to be funny, but at a time when fun carried no shame.

That was nice, but then our hunger returned. We came upon a grand hotel, as if in response.

There it was in sunny splendor – it was daytime now – a place anyone would be happy to have as a vacation destination.

Depleted as we were, Cornelia and I were taken aback by our luck. It felt like being launched on a honeymoon.

'This is such a sweet hotel,' said Cornelia, as we walked up the immaculate drive, the gravel graded, the grass edges clipped like an Army haircut and the maze, off to our right, not so much hedgerows kept in check as enigma in sculpted, bushy form.

'I wouldn't mind a try at that maze,' I murmured.

'You'd never get out,' she warned me. 'Then I'd have to find you.'

The car park was empty; that was a puzzler, like a surreal version of the maze – the one a tangle, the other a vacancy. Still, we found the heavy glass doors to the hotel open, and recently polished, for we were able to wave to our approaching selves in the reflective glass. We laughed at seeing windswept bums seeking to enter the fancy establishment.

'And we are minus luggage,' said Cornelia. 'They will think we are fugitives.'

'Or lovers desperate for a room,' I said. She was adjusting her hair in the providential mirror. 'I'm a wreck,' she sighed.

'You look as pretty as Margaret Sullavan,' I said.

She turned on me, so fast. 'How did you know? I love that woman to distraction.'

'*The Shop Around the Corner*,' I said. 'Who couldn't love her?'

'I've seen it eleven times.' It's funny how a movie can do that.

I was touched that both sisters had this thing for Sullavan. In this rush of amity, we entered the hotel. Perhaps it would be sweet for us. The extensive lobby seemed still and poised for business. The lights were on. A fire was burning in the display fireplace. There were Christmas decorations, with a floor-to-ceiling tree, so jolly and so carefully dressed we hardly appreciated that it was not Christmas, not in August, not even with 'Sleighbells' playing. The reception desk had a sign announcing itself but no one to receive us. Empty hospitality hung in the air with scented candles. We guessed there would be food somewhere, the stuff of brunches, banquets, tea dances and late night suppers.

We explored. There was a row of elevators. We ordered one and it was not as if the doors slid open to reveal a can of corpses or a sudden rush of blood. The empty elevator waited for us to enter. We declined (it did feel foreboding). Its doors slid shut and then it was up and away.

There was a pool in a courtyard with rows of recliners turned to face the sun, or angled for the shade, depending on your needs. There was a room-length bar, done in gold, its tidy bottles like the pipes and valves in some complicated piece of machinery, and all aglow, as if the bar itself might be tight and shining in its benevolent mood.

But there was no one to be found, not guests, not staff – not a ghost of a personage. A large hotel like this must have a great kitchen, with food in quantities that the three bears could live on forever. Cornelia called out for assistance but the sound of her voice trailed away in the lofty public rooms.

We were about to leave, when a door down a long corridor opened and a man appeared. He wore a black apron and carried a mop and a bucket. There was an unmistakable regret in his disapproving face that he had been cleaning a bathroom. He did not notice us at first, but then he stopped in his tracks.

'We're closed,' he called out, before we could speak. He stood still so it was incumbent on the two of us to approach him. He was losing his hair and clinging to dignity.

'Your front door was open,' I explained. 'We assumed this was a hotel.'

'Of course, it is,' said the man. 'What does it look like?' He had a name tag on his white shirt – Grady. 'But it's closed.'

'Is there a chance we could get something to eat?' asked

Cornelia. Grady did not answer, but he noticed scuffs of dirt on her blue suit. He took a white cloth that had been tucked in his belt and he started to dab at her lapels. 'You've got yourself in a mess, madam. Haven't you?'

'We have been walking for two days,' she said.

'Really? It looks as if you might have been... knocked about a bit by some... ruffian.' He peered at her so that he could dab more accurately. 'Yes, that's what it looks like. Does this gentleman prefer the rough stuff?' He looked at me with a blank expression, but then he winked and the wink was adhesive.

'Perhaps the lady would like to accompany me to a bathroom,' said Grady. 'We are fully equipped.'

'I thought the hotel was closed,' I said. I felt I needed to protect her.

Grady gazed at me in a mixture of weariness and irritation. Was I spoiling something? 'The bathrooms don't vanish just because it's out of season... sir,' he said in contained exasperation. 'After all, where am I or the caretaker meant to relieve ourselves? You can't overlook that.'

'Can we talk to the caretaker?' asked Cornelia.

'Out of the question. He's writing, isn't he? For all I know, he's writing us.' He giggled at his own joke. 'Quite the author, I can tell you. Bad-tempered, though. You know what writers are. He keeps an axe on his desk.'

'An axe? What does he write?' I wondered.

'Ghost stories. He talks to people you or I wouldn't see.' Grady looked around him, just in case, and his voice dropped to a whisper. 'He's not a well man, you know. I daresay I could do you a sandwich, for a modest consideration.' He looked at Cornelia. 'Tongue? Do you like tongue, madam?'

'I've never had it,' she answered.

'Oh, really,' said Grady, grave with disbelief.

* * *

And so we moved on leaving that begging hotel idle. But life for many of us can have the air of taking place in an abandoned hotel. You might imagine Texas's Chuck Whitman, one Chuck or another, counting the rooms in the establishment and contemplating his future. He did not know what to do to break his impasse, yet despite a headache, he sat down and wrote this on hotel letterhead paper:

'I do not quite understand what it is that compels me to write this. Perhaps it is to leave some vague reasons for the actions I have recently performed. I do not really understand myself these days. I am supposed to be an average reasonable and intelligent young man. However, lately I have been a victim of many unusual and irrational thoughts.'

Who doesn't know that stirring? So, as Chuck wrote out this letter he did not need to decide what to do. Yet he wrote the letter several times to get the spelling right and to say what he meant. Then he moved to another room and killed his mother and his wife, who were resting, after an afternoon walk, and then he went out for fresh air and killed fourteen others who had been playfully lost in the hotel maze.

FOUR

Being in Connecticut had accelerated my inclination towards absurd hopes and plunging disappointments. This was an old rhythm, but I knew enough to fear its pulse. In that flux I often forgot whether or not I had taken my own pills today. I could talk and answer questions; I had a reasonable survival intensity; I was hardly a danger to anyone; and I was doing my best, if you know what I mean. And I think I knew even then, in my bones or my synapses, that I might be safer yearning for Cornelia if never quite touching her. But yearning was building in me, like a plague.

'You look better today,' she said, without turning to me.

'In an odd way,' I told her, 'I wonder if this could be a healthy life.'

'If you can avoid the tongue sandwiches,' she said, and that let us chuckle together. Combinant orgasms are all very well, like fevered rallies in tennis, but one moment of laughing in unison may be as precious.

Lost in such thoughts, I had not noticed a shift in the terrain. It was flatter now, for we had stumbled upon the edge of a golf course. There is golf in Connecticut like squirrels; a sport built on frustration, a torture to the sane; an elusive skill to drive anyone mad. Above the long grass, I could see the upper halves of players and the swing of their sticks. Occasionally, there was that solid sound of contact – a good straight drive – and then the murmur of talk among the players.

We were at the 11th, the infamous Road Hole, a seemingly innocent par three, 211 yards, but a place where suicides and divorces were memorialized in a bronze plaque embedded in an oak tree at the tee.

'Do you notice,' I asked Cornelia, 'how the drive here flirts with that road – out of bounds?'

'Seems a foolish place to leave a road.'

'Or a perverse place for golf.'

'Don't you think golf finds perversity in any lie of the land?'

I agreed and I was confident enough to tell her this very dark story about another 11th (as I recall, somewhere in Scotland, I think it was near Inverary). A man had been playing the course there and after ten holes he was three strokes under par.

'Whatever that means,' said Cornelia loyally. Stroke is an imponderable word.

'Our man is feeling chipper. He sees glory if he can stay steady on the back half.'

'Sounds filthy,' she said, but she was interested. 'Is he wearing a kilt?'

'If you like. With gartered socks just below the knee. But he hooks his drive at the 11th,' I carried on. 'The ball flares out to the left, it bounces on the hard road and jumps up so violently that it crashes into the windscreen of a passing tour bus – it is a Catholic schools party on a day trip, abuzz with jollity, sandwiches and dirty jokes the Fathers can't help hearing.'

'You're making this up!' she accused me hopefully.

'It's too grim for that. The bus veers off the road and slides down an incline. It overturns. It catches fire. There are eleven deaths among the innocent, with four of them not yet confirmed in the Church.'

'You can't even keep a straight face,' she told me. 'You really are bonkers.'

'Have a little respect,' I implored her. 'I'm so close to tears. The wretched hooker goes back to the club house. He is shattered, distraught, at his wits' end, un-'

'I get it,' she snapped.

'He goes into the locker room, with its hushed and aghast assembly. He cries out to the heavens, "What, what should I do?" And a wizened man, the club professional, comes up to him and says, "Laddie, you have to keep your left thumb locked in by the right hand. It's the only way to fight a hook."'

* * *

Editor: Priceless! And you were not to know, but golf is my passion. There's nothing like bad taste for bringing people together. I'm encouraged by this, even if it's weird sometimes. But, you know, the troubled mind has become very viable lately.

Agent: Society is making progress?

Editor: We find that many readers are not entirely well, but more inclined to talk about it. They're drawn to the bipolar approach. We have a series of bipolar handbooks, you know: My Bipolar Vacation; Sex and the Bipolar Personality; Bipolar Investment.

Agent: I've seen some of those.

Editor: Steady backlist titles. We're doing a boxed set for Christmas. What we call in-house, 'Have Yourself a Horrid Little Christmas.' Our joke.

Agent: Don't you find the whole Happiness thing is passé?

Editor: Oh, one doesn't dare mention it now. Which raises an intriguing point. Our author?

Agent: Yes?

Editor: How is he? You can speak in confidence. He gets through his days? Do you think he could handle a tour? Breakfast TV

in Austin. A meet-and-greet in Waco? A karaoke reading in
El Paso?

Agent: I have every confidence. He travels well. He has his ups
and downs, you understand. I don't know the details. He likes
early bed, and early rising. Give him cheese whenever possible,
Sage Derby, with a little Glenmorangie. And marmalade in
the morning. But, look, this fellow sees the best part of four
hundred films a year. Doesn't that qualify as sane?

Editor: Not sure I could do it. But don't get me wrong. The
practical truth is that if our publicity people could alert the
media – discreetly, you understand – about the chance of
a little breakdown here and there – nothing drastic – that
might help. It goes with the book, if you know what I mean. A
gentle suggestion that he is... fragile? Brittle? Could build the
sympathy audience.

Agent: You would want him to act a little disturbed?

Editor: Not as such.

Agent: That might merit a little egging of the advance.

Editor: Not out of the question. But we might want to offset the
egg against the crack: it can cover the extra author insurance
we'll need.

* * *

We would have turned back, Cornelia and I, retraced our steps
and tried to make home before nightfall – if we still had a sure
sense of 'home' or direction in that lovely, aimless place. But we
were now in a part of the state that was laid out like a ceaseless
diversion, or a series of pregnant views. One tableau gave way
to another, not so much with a cut as a dissolve. And a dissolve
is beguiling and slippery; it is a current in the water that carries
you forward without any need for swimming. The things we
saw!

There was a dainty stone house on top of a hill. A prolonged exterior staircase gave access to it, and two men were laboring to carry a piano up those stone steps. They were an odd couple, the one lean, the other fat, one demure and the other bumptious. They both wore hats that kept slipping off their heads in the warmth and the exertion. The boxed piano was intact, but there seemed every possibility that it could be dropped and smashed into pieces on the climb. From a distance, this couple had the comic charm of men intent on a job of work but making a hash of it. Don't we love to watch such misadventures? It was as if they refused to notice how ill-suited they were, or how defeating their task was. They needed each other, and need is a first step towards neurosis.

So a stream ran on the far side of the hill with the staircase and the piano and the two stooges, and on its bank lounged a youngish man in austere dark dress while in the stream there was a beautiful younger woman, floating on her back, looking up, her mouth open, and holding flowers in one hand. Was she sleeping in the water, or was she drowned? I thought I heard a song on the wind, 'There's rue for you and here's some for me', unless it was leaves rustling in the air.

Cornelia looked at me with her black eyes. It seemed as if she was an undecided juror hearing my forlorn case.

'You'd like to make love to me, wouldn't you?' she asked, without relish or concern.

'Well...' I began. I could foresee so many counter-productive responses.

'You'd do it here? Now? In front of everyone?'

'Everyone?' I asked.

She made a shy nod over my shoulder, at the very audience I had taught her to appreciate in the wilderness of Connecticut. 'Wouldn't they be watching?' she whispered. 'I'm not sure I could bear that. Because if they're watching, I'd be watching, too. It's so hard to believe in yourself then. One wants to be natural. You see, it's lousy luck, but I may be a little… frigid. Is that the word?'

I was about to compile a catalogue of her assets and delights, but she had a lament she was determined to deliver.

'Something dreadful happened,' she declared. I did my duty: I begged her to tell me.

'A few years ago, in Britain, in Sussex, I met a man and I believed I was in love with him. You know that urging, I know you do. But I could not give myself to him, at least not in that mindless Irene-ish way.'

'Of course not.'

'Oh, don't pretend that isn't what men want. I'm sure you were pleased with it.'

'Well,' I struggled. 'She is an attractive woman.'

'She's a slut,' said Cornelia, as if that had been settled long ago. 'This hero of mine in Britain, he realized how timid I was and we happened to be on those high white cliffs to the east of Brighton.'

'I have seen pictures of them.'

'He asked if he could kiss me, and I said, only if we kept our eyes shut. I couldn't bear to see it as a real thing.'

I thought of saying, 'You are daft, my dear Cornelia', but this tale only made me want her the more, so I gave her a meek 'Yes?'

'He closed his eyes. I did the same. He reached forward. I waited to feel his mouth. Nothing. I waited. I thought I heard a splash far away. And when I looked – on my knees, I peered over the edge of the cliff; I was too faint to stand up – his body was floating in the sea. Quite dead, of course. Those cliffs are five hundred feet high.'

'That's terrible,' I said, though I was having to suppress the giggles, too. Tragedy and travesty are often tripping over each other.

'I haven't kissed anyone since,' she said. She drank a little of the water. 'I suppose I could try. Aren't you an authority on kissing?'

'On the screen,' I added. I could foresee a test coming.

'Well, you might try,' said Cornelia, in an uninterested way. 'We could pretend we're in a movie.'

Sooner or later, it comes to that.

'It would require cooperation,' I explained. 'Really, two people have to be active in it.'

'I see that in theory,' she admitted, but it sounded like a setback. 'I'm probably missing a chromosome, or something.'

'I doubt that,' I said valiantly, and although we were both sitting on the grass at the foot of a large tree, I leaned forward, and kissed her. It wasn't like splitting the atom, or being possessed by an immortal haiku. It wasn't even 'I've Got You Under My Skin'. But I used my tongue to open up her mouth, and I thought I felt that old tingle (I know it's not a very scientific word). Call it collusion or the swilling together of mouth waters.

'Did that do nothing for you?' I asked.

She reflected on it. 'Well, it wasn't insignificant, but what is it supposed to do?'

Cornelia was looking doubtful. 'Are they all watching me?' she asked. 'Are they paying attention?'

'There are always people watching,' I said. 'They like to watch. Let that be your energy, your inspiration. Think of yourself acting out the kiss.'

'You mean pretends?' I guessed we had come close to what she called her frigidity, her persona, and her reason for being in Connecticut now.

'How do you know?' asked Cornelia in wonder and I felt her hands at my face, drawing it towards hers. I had closed my eyes.

'I'm writing you,' I explained.

'You're as mad as a hatter,' she whispered, and kissed me. 'Again,' she said. Her mouth was like the Grand Canyon, or at least the Canyon de Chelly. And it was full of her as well as me.

* * *

That phrase, 'mad as a hatter', is said to derive from the use of mercury to treat the felt with which hats were made in the eighteenth century. The hatters, apparently, were at risk of absorbing enough of this mercury to hasten dementia. The hatting industry was once centred in Stockport in Cheshire and exporting six million hats a year by 1884. Charles Lutwidge Dodgson, otherwise known as Lewis Carroll, was born close to Stockport in 1832 and in 1865 he published *Alice in Wonderland*, which includes a character known as the Hatter.

I just mention this, but the hat is a neglected subject.

I would have said more, but then, as it happened, a drastic *now* intervened.

Associated Press, 14 December 2012: Breaking news arrives of a gunman or gunmen firing at an elementary school in Newtown, Connecticut... little is clear at first; it might all be a mistake. Other items on the same website: at the 13 December New York premiere of *On the Road*, Kristen Stewart 'went high fashion for the special screening event. She bared her firm midriff in a two-piece number under a see-through dress by Erdem with red pattern detailing. Looking sexy-yet-stylish, the brunette beauty arranged her hair into a simple ponytail and finished off the look with a pair of neon-colored pumps.'

This came in like any drab newsflash. I was writing this very book when the first word of Newtown appeared on the net. Naturally, my eye snagged on any mention of Connecticut. Then in the next few hours, the Newtown toll became clearer:

twenty-eight dead, twenty of them children aged six or seven, as well as the principal of the school, the killer and his own mother. There were rumors on the net that this young man, Adam Lanza, might be disturbed. But he had killed himself and his mother. So who could investigate that riddle?

INTERLUDE:
Margaret Sullavan in Connecticut

She was an enchantment by twenty-one, determined to rise above her own contradictions, and brave enough to try. So many loved her and that admiration was often too much for her. People called her Maggie – she encouraged it – she even suggested Madcap as a name. But she had been born a respectable Margaret, and she could play the Virginia society girl as well as an outlaw yielding to desire. She had a girl in her who entranced men and made them mad, as if they envied her unruliness. Some men loathe their own solemnity and long for its opposite. But then she could turn ladylike on a dime and tell the man – he might be naked in a hotel garden, erect, out of his mind over her – 'No, look, Jake, we must be sensible.'

At which, he hissed, 'I'm Jed, not Jake!', bewildered but vengeful, too.

She said, 'What?', and peered closely at the very lips that had been furious in their urge to kiss her. That voice of hers was renowned, haughty but fractured. Fools imitated her, but never got the real tremor. People would telephone her just to hear that voice. I did it myself. 'Hallo,' she sighed, and I put the phone down, trembling.

The voice was delicate but husky. She could still a packed theatre, sounding girlish or fragile, but on top of a maturity that was sometimes tragic. It broke your heart listening to her – if you were that way with voices.

But she was going deaf.

No one understood that. She seemed young and so perfect, even if she had an air that made people want to take care of her. But the deaf believe others are slurring and mumbling; their temper increases. She made fun of it, as a screwball confusion, the way she had married Henry Fonda because they were in a play together and kissing on stage, so what else was there to do?

That Fonda thing broke up quickly. It was a couple of months: the play ended and they had had sex a hundred times or so (who keeps count?). Henry emerged as an earnest fellow, prone to indignation, afraid he had been made the chump of his own desire. He disliked that more than not liking Maggie. They remained friendly; they got divorced like two people laughing over an automobile scrape, but passing on. Maggie was a risky driver, by the way. The divorce just enhanced her reputation for being emotional – or sexual. That was the screwball thing: the cheerful nuttiness was so attractive.

That's when she met Harris.

As he must have told her, he was the best stage director in the country then. Even if a play was feeble – especially then – he could do things with the actors that let you think you were watching Hamlet. *Harris had stealthy stage craft, like a thief taking a house at night. He made the stage feel like a movie. But his evil genius was getting into the souls of those people who have no course in life but to pretend, to lie professionally, to be actors. He was also handsome and ugly at the same time; people thought of Satan the moment they saw him, or realized he was gazing into them. He stared at people, like an animal; he never bothered with polite looking.*

He went after Maggie; lay in wait for her and trapped her in her corner. He stood very close to her, or in her emotional space. He took it over and she heard every word he said, though sometimes she seemed breathless. Had he taken her air as well as her space?

'Well, then,' he had said to her, the first time they met, when his eyes were about six inches from her. Nothing else, no introduction or small talk, but a kind of checking in, confirmation of arrival, prior to occupation.

'Yes, Jed,' is all she said and they were in bed in half an hour, locked in place. She fed on him; he taught her stuff the airy girl only thought she knew. Their adoration was flawless: she adored him, and he adored him.

Let's say he was physically infatuated with her – he believed in possession and the dry ground of an actress dependent on his watering interest. He talked to her in the third person, about how he had seen into the tricks she played to protect herself. He asked her to tell him about herself, and from that he fashioned a reading of her that would guide her as an actress – even to her own demise. That was his talent, letting other talent bloom, while teaching you that blooms must perish.

He could take an actress and explain her to herself with inescapable lucidity. Is that what I am? they'd be asking themselves. Is this my wreck? But then, like a torture master he'd educate them about their own bodies, in a contemptuous way, turning them round, taking them from the rear, listening to their gasping and not having to look at the astonishment in their faces – unless he did it in front of the mirror. He did that sometimes, so Maggie may have seen a beast in herself as well as his vulture head staring over her shoulder.

Women were in thrall to him for a season. And Maggie never fell so hard for anyone. Because he understood her need and played it with his cunning. But in that education, he taught her how lost she could be in hoping to be 'herself'.

Harris treated her the way he treated everyone – on the spur of his heartless mood. He lavished her with himself, then he withdrew. He was always taking over space. He filled her room with lilies while she was away – she could not get in the room;

but then he missed an appointment she had been counting on – and let her know it was deliberate.

She went back to Virginia, to try to get away, so he pursued her. Her family was horrified by him – they had never met a scoundrel before – but she saw that he was proof her people were idiots and Virginia a backwater. He had come after her. He had found her in life. He had uncovered her as an actress and as a female. She had given her consent, but it amounted to rape.

'I could live without you,' he told her once, just as she was coming: to see how she would react. But in the heat of the moment she misheard. She thought he said, 'I can't live without you.' And so in the agitated glow of her own coming – he was a master of timing on stage and off – she had realized, 'Jed, we're so special. No one understands us. We should do away with ourselves tonight.' It was her idea, yet his darkness often led up to murder or vanishing.

Maggie talked about this for a few days afterwards, while Harris rolled his eyes and stayed silent, like a director watching an actress going off on a mistaken tangent. She would come back, tired and more obedient. Harris gave orders or ultimata more than he explained, and Maggie's rare liberty liked to be driven by some tempest ringing in her ears.

She was of a mind and a kind of flight that longed to be directed, or written for. She knew that Harris had left his mistress, Ruth Gordon, and their son, apparently for her, for Maggie. Of course, you can argue, how could anyone as lovely and talented consider killing herself? But she saw what might be a pact, an ultimate embrace.

And you have to remember how, in the end, this Margaret Sullavan did kill herself – or let it happen.

You see, she was arrogant yet insecure, and people like that live on narrow ledges. Just before her end, she told a friend, 'I can't go on and I can't get out.'

That was later. In the meantime, perhaps because she recognized that Harris might destroy her, she decided she had to get away from him.

Well, she was cast in a picture, The Good Fairy, directed by William Wyler and it had a chance to be good. Willie Wyler was moved by her and he was touched when the cameraman told him sometimes she looked very good but then sometimes not so good.

'How's that?' asked Wyler, and the cameraman didn't know, but he thought it might be after Harris had telephoned her.

'She looks bad then?' asked Wyler.

'I'm not sure which is which,' said the cameraman. 'But there's a difference.'

Wyler tried to talk to Maggie; he was becoming very fond of her. But she stopped him; she put a cool hand over his mouth.

'Look,' she said, 'I think you ought to marry me. I have to get free from Harris. And marrying me wouldn't be so bad. Really, I can be very nice. And I like you so much, Willie.'

'Well, I could sure love you,' he told her. He was willing.

They became lovers – it's so natural if you're making a movie. But then one day, without warning, as they were shooting, Maggie looked horrified. As if she'd seen a ghost or a devil come to collect her. Harris had walked onto the set and he was staring at her from the dark beyond the light being filmed. That was a scene! They closed down for the day.

She was so scared. 'You have to marry me right now,' Maggie insisted to Willie and he did not argue. A few days later, there was a fight, in a garden in the rain, between Harris and Wyler, and Harris was defeated because he chose not to fight. Perhaps he thought Maggie would favor the loser. Maggie and Harris had a private meeting – who knows what they did? – but Maggie came out of the room and just told Willie, 'Come on!' They went to Yuma and got married. They fought and made up like kids for over a year, and then they divorced.

Time passed. Wyler would become an important director. He made a happy marriage with another actress, Margaret Tallichet, who gave up acting for him. His pictures included Dodsworth, The Letter, The Little Foxes, The Best Years of Our Lives, Roman Holiday *and* Ben-Hur.

Jed Harris's fame as a director remained (despite his enemies) and in 1938 he did an acclaimed first production of Our Town. *You had to see it, to be there as the hushed moments passed. He made pauses seem like melodies. Very soon after it opened, a Rosamond Pinchot killed herself. She was beautiful, wealthy and an actress who had been picked up by Harris. He had not cast her in* Our Town, *but she devoted herself to the costumes and being his lover. It was said that he then repudiated her. Unkindly. Some said she spoke of suicide and that Harris taunted her over the remark.*

Pinchot went home, parked her car in its garage, put a tube to the exhaust that would direct the carbon monoxide back into the car... and shut herself in. Harris's career diminished; so many people decided he was hateful. Still, he directed the original productions of The Heiress *and* The Crucible *(the latter in bitter dispute with its earnest author, Arthur Miller).*

After Wyler, Maggie made another film with Henry Fonda, The Moon's Our Home, *and they even talked about marrying again. She was all over the place, but then instead she married the agent and producer, Leland Hayward. They had two daughters and a son. She was a movie star and they were together for a decade (1937-47). There's a black-and-white photo of Maggie and Hayward in their garden in Brentwood; she's in a white bathing suit, stretched out, her eyes closed and he's kissing her upper breast. It's the best shot I ever saw of emotional bliss, and I hated them for it.*

That was their Californian life, where Leland needed to be an agent. But Maggie turned against Hollywood and bought a place in Brookfield, Connecticut: that was opting for the stage, the East, a classier life for the children. It was what she wanted, but impractical, and it made for trouble.

Maggie was always saying she wanted to be a wife and a mother – to play those parts. But in the mid-1940s, she had a big success on Broadway playing an actress in The Voice of the Turtle. *Sometimes she said she hated acting because it killed your own life, but then she said she loved it and needed it. When she went with* Turtle *to London, Hayward began to notice other women – he was an agent, after all.*

He was unfaithful, and she chose to see that as non-negotiable, when they still loved each other. So that marriage ended; he said it had been 'very irksome', as if to downplay the break-up. She wanted everything to stay nice, or enviable – like that photo! But in 1950 Maggie married again, to Kenneth Wagg, an Englishman who ran a malted milk company. It was foolish pride. She worked less, but on stage she was the deserted lover in Terence Rattigan's The Deep Blue Sea, *and then Sabrina in* Sabrina Fair *(by which time she was twenty years older than the part she was playing – yet no one seemed to notice the age gap; Maggie could persuade you and herself that she was a girl still).*

Margaret Sullavan was found dead in a hotel bed in New Haven, Connecticut, on 1 January 1960, that bad day for ledge-dwellers. I read it in the papers: shocking, but not a surprise. There were those who wondered whether she had ever seen Harris again. Let them wonder. Maggie died of barbiturate poisoning holding the script of a new play she was rehearsing, Sweet Love Remember'd. *(Don't forget the apostrophe.) She was fifty, and you heard her deafness was becoming an issue.*

Within a year, her younger daughter killed herself, aged twenty-one: it was that or an overdosed medication – the same as with Maggie. That child was thought to be ethereal, yet disturbed, by nearly everyone who met her. She had spent time in clinics with some kind of fits. What does it do now to say there was this turmoil in Maggie? And how does one reconcile that fearful history with a handful of her films that can still make you feel alive? The pretending lasts longest, crystal clear, after the real lives have been hung up in history.

PART II

PART II

FIVE

I don't know how it happened. Was there really some Satan, some Jake or Jed, a wolf prowling through the woods of Connecticut, pursuing romance?

If the attack happened in my sleep, did I dream it, thinking of kissing Cornelia? Or is it possible that I did it, and she was too tactful to mention that? When I awoke, there she was, her suit a little more torn and spoiled, perhaps, sitting against a tree, smoking a cigarette. I hadn't realized she used cigarettes.

'What happened?' I wondered. The early morning seemed warm already until you felt a coldness close to the ground. There was dew on the grass and a scuffle of footprints in it.

'Two men,' she told me, 'I didn't get their numbers. They came by in the night. You were fast asleep.'

You know how it is when you wake up and a dream you had is running out on you? Somehow my head was so muddled. I could remember no action, just the reproach in Cornelia's pale face, gazing into my sleep, her mouth opening and closing. Had she been screaming?

'What happened?'

'What do you think happened?'

'You should have called out.'

'I did. Nothing woke you.'

I didn't know what to say and she must have seen the confusion on my face. I think to the best of her ability she had reached a certain abstract fondness for me.

'Don't look so sad,' she told me. 'It would have been worse if I'd been a person. When you're a character it's only a scene, isn't it? This might get cut in the end.'

'How can you say that? What do you mean?'

'I mean that the author will determine it all, whether I'm going to be raped, whether it should be recounted in simple or immense detail, and what it amounts to afterwards. It's hardly personal, is it? Nothing is in my life. I've done stand-out scenes in my time – they vanished. You see, I was just sent here because I was caught up in a mad story. Just make the best of yourself in Connecticut, they said.'

'But then two strangers come along and rape you? That's hardly fair.'

'What else can we expect? We're not responsible.'

I nearly laughed out loud, 'But, of course, you are. We all are.'

'Not really,' said Cornelia. 'I have no say in these things. You describe me as a frigid woman, so you decide I don't love you, or couldn't. Isn't that right?'

'Well, I have to keep the story moving along. I have an agent and a publisher will be down on me if I don't.'

'Your having me say I'm frigid has more to do with you than me,' she said. 'Honestly, I'm a prisoner. I have no energy of my own. Don't they always say that about the insane – they're not responsible? I'm no better than a wild cat you pick up and you look into my eyes and either you see wisdom, or fury; affection or hatred.'

She seemed tired, yet unaffected by the rape. She was like an actress playing that part, or a cartoon character, shattered one moment and then whole again. If you're raped eight performances a week, you need to pick up a certain professionalism. That aplomb must have many adherents in Connecticut, who meet any reasonable definition of 'mad', or whatever word you care to use. I see that Yale itself is calling for papers for a conference, 'The Varietal Definitions of Insanity and How a Disturbed Person May Negotiate That Maze' (it is co-chaired by Professor Emeritus Edward Zigler and Joyce Carol Oates). There is a picture with the brochure, not well reproduced, but I think it is Jack Torrance clutching his axe on which the blood itself is freezing slowly in the maze at the Overlook.

'But we kissed,' I insisted.

A look of half-forgotten ease skipped through her face like a cloud across the sun, 'Oh right, was that us?'

'What flavor was the kiss?'

'Gin?' she guessed.

I was touched by that much proof. My grandmother drank gin until ninety-three and she let me sip it once as a child. I could not imagine a greater gulf between enticing aroma and disgusting taste. Grandma laughed and I saw the flare of yellow-brown in her white hair – it was a white that had been red once. She smoked persistently and a couple of times set her clothes or an armchair on fire. Of course, she was warned that the habit was bad for her, but she lived on, laughing.

'You look sad still,' said Cornelia.

'I was thinking about Newtown,' I said. 'It's not far from here.'

'What is that?' She had the air of a child being queried about a large issue in which she had no stake or comprehension.

'The deaths of the children at the school.'

'I don't know about that.'

I was at a loss. 'Surely everyone knows.'

She could see my disbelief, and the first intimation that she might not be simply self-centred, deaf and sleeping, but an alien creature who could not grasp history or breaking tragedy.

'Newtown,' I said. 'You have not heard about the killing of twenty-six children?'

'Was there a fire?' Cornelia asked.

'A young man came to the school and shot them.'

'How? Why?'

'He used his mother's gun.'

Cornelia was in tears. It was not just the story itself, but the revelation of 'facts' of which she had been unaware. She felt ashamed, as well as desperate for the children.

'They were aged six and seven,' I added.

'Why would he shoot them?'

'They say he was mad,' I said.

'People always say that,' said Cornelia. 'It doesn't help.'

'Because the killer had guns, I suppose. I believe the weapons all belonged to his mother.'

'What did she say?'

'Nothing,' I said. 'He shot her, too.'

Cornelia was shaking, this slim fashion plate who frequented parties where scavenger hunts required 'forgotten men'. So I told her as much as I knew, and her face was so open I seemed to be pouring water into dry earth. And yet, within mere minutes, I discovered that Cornelia was forgetting essential details of the story. I filled her up with it, but there was some leak in her system. The knowledge ran through her. Later that day, it was still as if I was telling her for the first time.

'How long have you been in Connecticut?' I asked her.

'I don't know. You lose track of time. But I remember one thing about when I came, I asked myself would good times ever come back again.'

'Good times?' Hardly anyone used that term any longer.

'The depression, the poverty, will there be a war?' she asked. 'Just the fear itself.'

* * *

'Is that gunfire to the north?' Cornelia asked me.

'Which way is north?' I said.

'There's the sun setting,' she said, looking at the glare. 'Can't you work out the direction?'

'I am hopeless at that,' I said, so I thought I'd ask her, 'Would you like to kiss again.'

She shook her head. 'I don't think so. Remember, please, I was just raped.'

Then another rumble could be heard. Closer? 'I think that *is* gunfire,' I admitted. 'But it's far away.'

Cornelia nodded and stared towards her north. 'Still, if you can hear it, it must be close enough. Is it artillery or bombs dropping?'

'That's thunder,' I said. I hoped to reassure Cornelia.

'If that was thunder why isn't it as humid as wet blankets?' was all she said. There are people who can drive you mad if you try to look after them.

Whatever the noises were to the north, and whether it was the north or just jazz in the air picked up by troubled heads, it was a splendid evening in this part of Connecticut. The air was warm, to be sure, but as Cornelia had observed it lacked that clammy weight of unexpressed moisture, the humidity that may have given pioneers doubts at first in New England.

And as the moonlight came up, the forest was an enchanted place: it reminded me of stage shows – Hansel and Gretel, perhaps, as if staged by Max Reinhardt himself – when the ominousness of night was held back by a stage lighting in which one could see enough to feel blessed. Times are hard and likely to get harder, but I have always enjoyed the story of a boy and a girl, lost to the world, until they find each other and that old mercy falls on them. They are in love. Their bliss is so intense, so captivating, they do not notice they are prisoners in a gingerbread Treblinka.

'Look,' said Cornelia, 'aren't those people over there?'

The moon had fallen on the frilled white dress of Susan Bone, sitting on a mossy bank. Then the dark hump next to her started to move and I realized it was her David Bone, with a butterfly net over his head. Or was he wearing it as a hat?

'Dr Bone,' I called out, trying not to give way to naked relief at finding someone in authority.

'Good Lord!' he cried, looking up. 'There you are! We knew you would be somewhere. We weren't too worried yet.'

'Oh, really?' said Susan Bone. 'I would have called it worried. I would have called it flat-out afraid for your job if you lost any more patients.'

'Don't listen to her,' Bone told us. 'It's just her giving me the needle.'

'Well, I like that,' cried Susan in a pique that did not seem playful. 'Is that your subtle way of saying I've been on the smack again, just taking a little afternoon sip of laudanum, or disappearing with a syringe of morphine? Just because I can hear the sad foghorn of the ships, my dear, drifting over the Sound, and cannot shrug off the melancholy, the grief, of all that has passed –'

'Oh, Susan, snap out of that Mary Tyrone stuff,' said a weary Bone. 'We are looking for Baby, if you recall.'

'Of course, we are,' she said, and in a trice she shifted from being the dismantled older woman to a smart young thing scouring the woods of Connecticut for an escaped feline, lithe but on the large side.

'Have you two seen Baby?' she demanded of us.

'Baby is a mature leopard,' added David. But she was back at him, with, 'Oh, David! I don't see how a leopard can ever be regarded as "mature". They are wild things and impetuous; they are not like us.'

'If one of them lands on your back, claws exposed to get

a grip, you'll know what "mature" means, my good woman. Mature is over 150 pounds of muscle and the ability to move at 35 miles per hour if it is worried about being late.'

'I don't think leopards – certainly not Baby – ever worry,' she said with authority.

'Well, bully for Baby,' said David. 'I wish I was him.'

Susan was coquettish now. 'You do? Leaping on my back. Mauling me, your good woman? Having your way with me?' She looked up at Cornelia and me. 'Alas, we are not quite alone. Another time.'

David Bone was extricating himself from the net on his head. 'I hope this isn't damaged,' he said, examining the pattern of holes tied together with white string. 'Dr Darkbloom will never forgive us if it is. We just grabbed it on the way out.'

'When you're tracking leopard, even if they're immature, or downright silly,' said Susan, 'speed is of the essence.'

'Here in Connecticut?' I asked – someone had to say it. 'A leopard?'

'It can happen,' she said. 'Traveling menageries with lazy keepers. A zoo hit by a hurricane. And some people keep them as pets and reckon everything is under control, until the leopard gets the scent of nature in its nostrils. My aunt had an ocelot in Old Saybrook. Everything was hunky-dory until overnight that ocelot became a raging demon. Once an ocelot, always an ocelot. That's what I say.'

I was amused, but when I looked at Cornelia, I could see that she was troubled. Was it by the ease and teasing of their emotions, the mere hint of big cats at liberty, or the after-echo of that gunfire?

'Shuttlecocks,' whispered Cornelia, just like that, as if she had remembered something she needed to get at the shops.

'Do you play?' asked Susan. She had the limber air of being good at most games.

'I beg your pardon?'

'Badminton. We have a net in our garden, you know. It's a gentle game: exercise without hostility, I love the massive effort and then the feathery flight of the thing.'

'Susan was a State finalist a few years ago,' Bone reminded us.

'Thank you for remembering that, David,' said Susan at her most imperious. Her head tilted back so that the line of her nose was nearly horizontal. A pea could have sat there without moving. Cornelia seemed more hunched than she had been and her gaze was fixed on the ground in front of her. It was shyness verging on catatonia.

'Cheer up,' I said, and I took her cold hand. She snatched it back but then she smiled a little as if realizing what I was attempting.

'Shuttlecocks,' she whispered again, apologetically.

'Exactly,' I said, though I had no idea what that quaint word signified. Screwball and shuttlecocks – there should be a prize! (If you can hazard an answer, do write in. You're not helpless!)

Well, the four of us began to walk back through the lustrous twilight. I say 'back' because David Bone had said something about going home, and I think we all felt ready for that, and trusted his sense of direction.

I found myself side by side with Bone. 'You realize,' he said, 'we haven't had our sit-down yet.'

'What is that?'

'Well, I like to spend some time chatting with newcomers before they get acclimatized to our place. Get the record straight. Symptoms. Case history, education, hobbies, allergies, stuff like that. Nothing to be alarmed about. We might do it tomorrow. I'll make a pot of coffee – or perhaps you'd prefer something stronger?'

'Coffee would be admirable,' I said.

'Really? It's not supposed to be good for us, you know.'

I thought I would offer a pleasantry. We seemed to be getting on so well. 'Neither is the sound of gunfire in the distance.'

'Ah!' He looked up. 'Military exercises, I wouldn't wonder,' said Bone. 'Now that Washington seems to have got the message, there seems to be some preparing going on.'

'What message is that?' I wondered. But before the doctor could fill me in on the current situation, the headlights of an old Dodge wagon came rolling over the hillocks in front of us. The car was just ploughing through the country, as if being pursued. But the driver saw us, and pulled to a halt for news. The wagon was bulging with family, and the roof had several possessions on it – a rocking chair, two battered suitcases, a tuba, and a dog, a mutt, who seemed quite trusting about this means of traveling.

'Any sign of them hereabouts?' the driver asked.

'Who?' said Bone. 'Who's who?'

The driver said his name was Pop Horton. He and his family were hightailing it to get away from the damn Martians.

'We don't have Martians hereabouts,' said Susan. 'We don't play fast and loose with our property values, Mr Horton.'

Horton blinked several times. Susan was nothing like any danger he had expected to meet. Yet no one – not even a passing Pop Horton – could fail to see the outline of challenge on her.

As was his wont, and his vocation, David tried to sort the matter through. 'Now, tell me old chap – you did say Martians?'

'You got that right, captain,' agreed the driver. 'Heard on the radio, they've landed over in New Jersey and coming this way. They got machines with searchlights and ray guns, stuff you never heard of.'

'On the radio?' said Bone.

'That's what I said!'

'Are you sure you're not having your leg pulled?'

At that moment a young man so large and so dressed in white he resembled a cloud, but a cloud with black olive eyes, came tottering over the rise. 'Mr Horton!' he cried out between gasps – he was not in the best condition. 'I have to tell you – the Martians...'

'You seen 'em?' asked Horton. I saw he had a vintage rifle beside his seat. Lee-Enfield, I fancied, circa 1917.

'No, and no one ever will,' declared the young man. 'It was a feeble jest, you see.'

'Jest?'

'Yes.' The olive eyes fluttered as the cloud struggled for air. 'It was just a game at the expense of all these invasion scares. We were doing *The War of the Worlds* as a little play – perhaps you know it? – quite good still.'

'Never heard of it,' said Horton. He would no more let his suspicions go than he would have wiped away a grievance.

'Anyway,' said the cloud, 'I'm just trying to find everyone who believed in it, put their minds at ease and ask them please to go home. You know, I have a feeling we're in Connecticut by now.'

'Connecticut!' cried Horton in honest terror. For that was worse than Martians. 'We're there?'

'I believe so.'

'You most certainly are,' said Susan, a home-state booster. 'Smell that air!'

Horton was in a fix now, caught between a possible alien onslaught and the legend of Connecticut as the haven for loonies.

'There ain't no invasion?' he demanded.

'Of course not!' said Bone.

'Not yet,' promised the cloud.

'Well, all I can say,' began Pop Horton.

'Yes?' said Susan.

'There are some pretty crackpot folks out for a midnight picnic.'

'Wouldn't that have been a lovely idea?' said Susan. 'David, you didn't bring sandwiches, did you? Smoked salmon?'

'No, dear,' said the doctor. 'I think Baby wolfed them down before I could pack. We were tracking Baby, you remember?'

'Oh,' she said, accepting a courtly kiss on the hand from the cloud. 'He'll come home when he's ready. He always does. Baby knows which side his bread is buttered.'

SIX

No one at The Retreat cared to talk about the troubles. Yet one corner of the building was plainly damaged by what could have been artillery fire. I bumped into one and two (they were delivering a newcomer, a Lady Eve Sidwich, who insisted her arrival was a silly error that would be settled as soon as she could talk to 'someone in charge'). One and two no longer recognized me. They seemed so busy. But I pointed out the damage to the house. They said there had been a storm, one of those sudden Connecticut gales, like a seizure in the atmosphere. So much for happy days and blue nights.

I was about to remonstrate with them when Irene appeared. She was wearing tennis whites and carrying one of those old-fashioned wooden rackets. She never noticed me, but fixed on Lady Eve.

'Do you play tennis?' she demanded of the new arrival.

'Not since I was a girl in Tunbridge Wells,' said Eve.

'We could find you some gear,' said Irene, 'and there's a court free. We might just have time. I haven't had any exercise all day.'

She did notice me then. 'Oh, there you are,' she said, 'I was wondering what had happened to you. Did you rescue Cornelia? How gallant of you. Look, while her ladyship is changing, we could renew acquaintance if you'd like. I think we could squeeze it in.'

So it worked out. While the Lady Eve was accommodated in one changing room, in another Irene swiftly took me without removing her whites. As ever, she was intense and extraordinary, if forgetful.

'You're in love with Cornelia, then?' she demanded as she plunged through my feeble edifice and did her best to hurry.

'Well,' I said. What could I say?

'On your own head be it,' she said. But then she gasped and gave herself over to her pleasure. She had scarcely recovered from her rapture, with me a heap of discarded clothes on the floor, when the Lady Eve's fine contralto rang out, 'Ready when you are!'

'I have to rush,' said Irene. 'But I'll catch you later. Of course, Cornelia can never do this, you realize. It's just eternal, baleful contemplation with her. Bit of a bore.'

I heard that Irene whipped the Lady Eve 6-1, 6-2 and prompted comparisons with Helen Wills herself, who by then had seven US Nationals and eight Wimbledons.

They were off and playing by the time I tottered out of the changing room. I could hear the smack of balls and their cries of wonder in the distance.

Whereupon, a suspicious fellow came up to me. There was a look of anger or anxiety on his face. He was staring in the direction of the sounds of tennis. 'The same dame,' was all he would say.

'Which one?' I asked.

'The card-sharp on the ship,' he said, as if I hadn't been paying enough attention. But I can only do so much, and I really don't recall a ship. Still, I did get a replenishing lemon barley water for the demolished Lady Eve.

'How frightfully kind,' she said. 'Your friend is so swift, and you know I could have sworn she'd just had a roll in the hay! How does she do it?'

I was not the one to explain that, certainly not when I caught a glimpse – it was like picking up a disease called regret – of

Cornelia, crouched in a corner, gazing at me, like a hurt kid who had been left out of the game.

'It was only yielding to instinct,' I tried to explain to her.

'It doesn't matter,' she said, in her woeful way. 'Though I could kill Irene sometimes. If that's why I need to be here, it's hard to have her here too.'

Dwelling on these issues, I found myself in the spacious consulting rooms of Dr Bone. He had room for a wet bar and a pool table, as well as the requisite elements of his professional office, including the proverbial couch, an inviting and ample piece of furniture with cushions and a large coverlet done in Turkish designs. I was headed for the couch as my designated spot when David Bone, as bouncy as a kid, threw himself on it first and put his hands behind his head. He was all smiles and in possession.

'You take the armchair,' he said. 'It's very comfortable. I've had a few patients doze off on the couch.'

'Of course,' I said, trying to be agreeable. 'I just assumed the couch might be for me.' There are things one has looked forward to.

'I like to take a different tack.'

'May I ask,' I said, 'are you Freudian?'

'Well, yes and no,' said Bone in the manner of a man who welcomed a good discussion. 'Of course, I couldn't be happier that we've got the old boy out of Vienna, even if that probably means we're going to be deluged with European shrinks. I don't know if America will be able to provide enough patients for them all.'

'There seems no danger of that,' I offered.

'Maybe not,' said Bone, cheerily. 'Anyway, I read him all the time. He's as good as a detective story sometimes. But he does go off the deep end. Seems to think, finally, that everyone's sick. Can't fathom that: if everyone's sick, no one is – take my point? So I mix it up a bit – Freud and Will Rogers, if you know what I mean. I wept for two days when the old Okie got it at Point Barrow (an airplane crash). Cherokee on both sides, you know. They asked him, "Did his ancestors come over on the *Mayflower*?" He said, "No, they met the boat!" How do you like that?'

Then he seemed to remember me. 'You see,' he said, 'I take the couch for two good reasons. One: it's not what you expected – surprise is the best way into the unconscious. That's basic Bone. Two, doing this all day I get very tired and twenty years in a desk chair has given me a nasty back condition. It was Susan's idea, that I deserved the couch. She's brilliant, you know. Out of her mind some of the time, and it's best not to talk to her too much, but an original thinker.'

'Plus a vivid character,' I agreed.

'You've put your finger on it there. Makes me think we'll get on like a house on fire. That reminds me, if you hear a fire alarm, don't be worried. It goes off of its own accord. Something in the wiring. Nothing anyone can do about it. Two alarms – still no problem. Three and you should run for your life.' He considered and started another round of laughter. 'Of course, probably too late by then. You're toast and counting!'

'We live on a perilous edge,' I said. But David Bone seemed comfortable and ready to attend to my case.

'Very well,' he said, 'tell me your sad story. In your own way, but not too sad, please. It's a positive ending we're going for. If I close my eyes, just carry on. I'll be digesting it all, making notes in my head, as it were. I don't like to take notes while you're talking – could start you thinking you're someone in a book. Then you'd never stop.'

'Well...,' I tried to begin. I stumbled through the elementary facts: the father who went away one morning and... the mother in jail... life as a merchant seaman, and my unfailing seasickness... awkward romantic misadventures... the unfortunate matter in Bend, Oregon... discovering that my sister was in an asylum...

'Aha!' cried Bone. 'Look, old boy, I won't beat around the bush. But this kissing thing of yours – what do you think that means?'

'The big lips collision?'

'That very thing. Sounds intriguing.'

'Mouths melting together?'

'I'll say.'

'Tongues alone at last?'

'Hey, give me a break!' he cried. 'You're getting me hot and bothered already.'

'You mean, why am I writing about it?'

'In a nutshell, yes.'

I folded my arms and leaned back, as if to give the impression of judicious survey. But I will admit I was taken off guard. There had been an occasion in my life when a stranger took it into her head – indeed, sucked me into that place – by kissing me repeatedly in a parked car at night. This was on a country lane, all dark, with the smells from a nearby farm. It was a rapture that came and went. No more, no less.

'Can't get enough of it, I suppose,' I admitted to Bone.

'Aha,' he said, 'Now we're getting somewhere.' But he never said where, or how to come back.

'Do you regard it as an illness?' I asked him. 'A mania?'

'Well, I wonder.'

An idea came into my head. Assuming this was circa 1940, and he was a fashionable practitioner in Connecticut, 'Did you ever kiss Margaret Sullavan?' I asked, assuming she had been in and out of treatment.

'Not that I recall,' said Bone. His eyes opened and he sat up on the couch. 'That reminds me. Want to hear a story?' he asked, and I guessed there was no stopping him.

His enthusiasm was daunting yet inspiring. If that sounds hard to fathom, try a few sessions of the Bone method. I noticed Irene out on the lawn. She was wearing an ivory evening gown now, and as she saw me through the window she made a slow, lewd gesture for me that I am not going to describe here.

'So, there was this boy. He lived in, let's say, Fresno or Duluth or Burlington – it doesn't really matter. Lived with his Mom and his Dad. He was an only child. Get the picture?'

I nodded; it was all I had to do.

'They're not poor, but they're far from rich. So the boy goes to school, he's nine, let's say.'

'Not eleven?' I asked.

'Funny you should say that,' said Bone. 'I was going to say eleven. Let's compromise on ten. Well, one day he walks home from school, lets himself in the house, it's not locked, and calls out to his Mom, the way he always does.

'Nothing. No reply. This is very unusual. She's always there with a cooked tea for him – a kipper, eggs and bacon, a pork pie. So he waits and he makes himself a dripping sandwich. It starts to get dark. Then his dad comes home – as usual.

'The boy says, "Dad, where's Mom?"

'The father looks about the house – not a big house – two up, two down – and he says, "Well, I don't know, lad. She'll be here soon. Off on some errand, I expect".

'Time passes. Dad gets the supper. The boy's worried by now, but Dad says, "Oh, she's all right. She'll be here before long." But they go to bed, and she's still not back.

'Next day, the boy doesn't know what to do. Dad says, "She'll be home later today, I'm sure of it." The boy goes off to school. Comes home. No one. Not a soul. Dad gets home, and he says, "Well, it beats me. Don't know what could have become of her".

'Mom never comes home. Life goes on. Year or so later another woman moves into the house. The kid doesn't like her, but she gets his tea. He grows up. Goes away. Goes off to college to the other side of the country. Becomes – oh, let's say, a palaeontologist. Makes a career and a life for himself. Doing well. Married. A kid of his own. Hardly ever hears from his Dad.

'One day he gets a letter from a lawyer in, wherever it was…'

'Fresno or Duluth,' I remind him.

'Or it might have been Burlington. The letter says, "Regret to inform you, but your Dad passed away last Thursday. Not much of an estate. I'll send you the papers. Just one question – what are we going to do with your mother?"

"The son writes back, "What mother?"

'And the lawyer sends him another letter saying that his mother has been in an asylum in Fresno or whatever for nineteen years. His Dad had her committed there and never said a word. What do you think of that?'

'It's hard to believe,' I said – and it was.

'But it happened to a fellow I know, a Dr David Bone.'

'What did you do?'

'Ah,' he said, 'what would you have done? Just wanted you to have a sense of where I'm coming from. After all, if I'm going to be any help to you, you need to understand me. Right?'

It was not what I had expected, and yet I felt relieved as a child does when he or she has a satisfying story read aloud. I agreed with myself to leave the matter open as to whether Dr David Bone was a genius, a fraud or just cheerfully scatterbrained. In that last respect, the temperature of mood is so important.

Outside Bone's office, I looked up and saw a gaunt young man, leaning against the doorpost of a low-slung cabin in a sunless twilight, feeding himself crackerjack, steeped in loneliness and practicing the sound of his mother's voice. Was he waiting for his appointment with Bone? In that light, I could see that he might be melancholy, and driven to fill his isolation with melodrama. A fellow like that could be unpredictable, even if he did seem a nice guy, normal, but tall and lean, and willing to share a supper of milk and sandwiches.

When this young man realized I was watching him, he gave me a boyish grin as if to say sometimes a guy had to do some odd things to help the time pass.

'Talking to myself,' he called out and I waved my hand in acknowledgement. He was someone you wanted to like. I'm sure you know that quality of yearning neediness. It's hard to pass by.

So I concluded that, whatever his unusual methods, Dr Bone might give good couch, compelling stories and something to laugh at. In telling the strange tale of the Fresno kid he had managed to convey a resilient humor beneath it all. I did not feel cast down.

I next discovered that in a secluded chalet attached to The Retreat there were three critically wounded inmates who had been hurt in the earlier damage. This was much more than wind. From a brief survey I guessed that random long-range artillery had had a lucky hit, or was it an intended warning? There was no reliable news to say how the disturbances were advancing, or how serious they might be – but nothing was more disturbing than that uncertainty. One began to note the surreptitious wearing of shoulder-strap boxes containing gas masks. I was struck by how devoutly Connecticut seemed to be living in the crisis of the late 1930s. How much the black rubber reminded me of a death mask. Surely, nowadays, we would have painted comic faces on the masks to keep the children entertained.

But then, to disarm every foreboding, a great and authentic storm began to arise. Again, there had been no warning. But the birds in the air were just as unprepared and I swear I saw a few of them – cardinals and swallows – blown backwards in the draft. Then gray gulls arrived, screaming, torn and outraged, hurled in by some convulsion at the shore.

* * *

Editor: So, this war we're getting?

Agent: A bad show.

Editor: Just clue me in – which war?

Agent: You must remember that in 1940 and '41, this world was anticipating war, sometimes in the craziest ways.

Editor: And, of course, once we get into our Connecticut we realize that there's arrested development going on – everyone there thinks it is the eve of the Second World War.

Agent: Or III or IV.

Editor: Yes, I do feel that our author is saying this could also be the brink of our war. A new, 2023 war?

Agent: I know he's sensitive to that.

Editor: And – here's a plus – this modern war has a distinct weather feel. I like that a lot. People are ready for the weather angle now.

Agent: I'm sure that's so.

Editor: Play it lightly, though, I think. Not to be heavy-handed.

Agent: I'll pass that on.

Editor: Fascinating that Margaret Sullavan thread – the way show people were then. Personally, I cherish the old pictures. Harris – never heard of him before.

Agent: A lord in his time.

Editor: So I gather. Might be a part for Cumberbatch.

Agent: You're thinking a movie?

Editor: You never know. Options always open.

Agent: They knew how to do it then.

Editor: Didn't they? So, I think I'm having the lapin chasseur. What about you?

SEVEN

'I don't believe this was foreseen,' said David Bone, looking at the weather. As the wind grew stronger and brought its own gift, a horizontal rain that lashed as much as it drenched, he was hunting for shutters for the clinic windows. But some were painted over and immovable, while others fell off like dead teeth as soon as they were opened. 'Golly,' he said. And Susan, at his side, added, 'Golly gee'. Of course, I did not know Connecticut fully, not then, so I imagined this was simply a late summer storm, nudged on by a Gulf hurricane – could it be Emilie or Eleanor? But as I watched the Bones I guessed that this weather was out of the ordinary. An entire shrub – azalea, perhaps – flew past us, like a wig that had quit its wearer.

I was with Bone, waiting for his orders. It was his clinic, and he was the chief of staff of Connecticut's psychotherapeutic defenses. I trusted him to know what to do. If I and others had been brought here to Connecticut, because of our frailty, our turmoil and our neurotic reluctance to reach decisions, surely the man in charge must be in charge.

'Should we call the Governor?' said Bone. 'Or the President?'

'The lines are down,' wailed Susan.

I was going to say, 'Use email?', but by then I realized how easily a chance remark, a general wish to be useful, could only add to the estimate of my disturbed state. At that moment, a muddied leopard, its fur in shock from the rain, its wild being doused in fear, slouched across the lawn and set itself at Susan's feet, whimpering. It was Baby come home, a shadow of his old self.

'I suppose it's global warming,' I said, and Baby looked up at me, a leopard of woeful countenance and discarded ferocity. He wanted to be a domestic animal now.

'What on earth is that?' demanded Bone. 'This is no time for more mumbo-jumbo.'

In a profuse and increasingly rowdy hurricane (they would name it Alexandria), I was not inclined to get into that controversy, especially with people who felt that weather was in the lap of the gods, so leave it there. These people thought that nature was real, observable and mundane, and they believed that weather was pretty and swell most of the time, yet capricious and always poised to spoil a parade.

We did what we could. As flooding began, we escorted chattering patients to upper floors. Where a few windows had been beaten in by gale force or the flapping percussion of useless shutters, we put up tarpaulins and even bed linen, though that usually ripped in a few minutes. Dr Bone was an indecisive tower of strength; he issued every order and instruction with military emphasis, specially those that contradicted orders he had uttered moments before. Susan Bone was an endless supply of towels and tissue paper for drying our rain-spattered spectacles. Cornelia and Irene found a semblance of sisterhood in making hot chocolate in an upstairs kitchen.

'I don't know what this is going to do for our Conference,' said Bone as we ducked to avoid flying tree limbs.

'Conference?' I asked. This was as new to me as global warming had been to him.

'It's only a few weeks away. "Is Insanity in the Constitution?" is the topic this year. We have a couple of the Supreme Court fellows scheduled. National coverage. Part of Connecticut Mental Health Awareness Month. Funny thing, there I was wondering if war would get in the way of it, but I never reckoned on this.'

'War?' I said. Was this some explanation for the gunfire we had been hearing?

'Czechoslovakia, Sudetenland, Abyssinia,' he said. 'Take your pick.'

It was hard to find a bright side, but still the sounds of the storm – like an amateur production of *King Lear* – brought a furtive smile to the gloomiest eye. We are perverse enough to find something comic in catastrophe. We can always say it is our craziness showing.

* * *

One night later, around 3.11, there was a fearsome sound, a rushing in the air above us, but then it became like a convulsion generated by the clinic itself, as if possessed. In the first seconds of being awake I wondered if a power system in the basement had exploded or gone rogue. Or was it some historic bedlam that wanted vengeance? But when I walked out of my room into the corridor, though the air seemed to be vibrating still, there was no sign of smoke.

A couple of fellows appeared, as if on duty, but caught playing cards. They might have been twenty-one and twenty-two.

'What happened?' I said.

Twenty-one ignored me and pushed me aside, but twenty-two stopped for a moment, and told me, 'Probably a reconnaissance fighter plane, low level.'

'Reconnaissance?' I said. 'For what?'

'They'll only know if they find something, won't they? Stands to reason.'

'But the disturbance,' I complained. 'Everyone will be awake and anxious.'

'Little bit of the passive aggro,' said twenty-two. 'Nice knowing you.' I noticed that he was carrying an automatic rifle against his leg. So it was not obtrusive – but inside the clinic! This left me feeling that there might be more going on than was being admitted.

As I stepped outside the clinic and onto the lawn, it happened again. I did not so much see the plane as feel the thunder and the shock of it passing – the WOW! and the WHAM! I felt that if I had been wearing a hat it would have been removed – and though I seldom wear hats, don't assume I have forgotten them as a promised subject. The noise was not just great, or deafening, or whatever – it was not a matter of decibels – it was the authority of the surveillance and the overflight that was crushing and appalling. There may be no need to bomb anywhere when aircraft can be flown over a population at a couple of hundred feet. Do that a few times and resistance will be gone.

Susan was there. I saw her, though I had to clear my eyes of tears.

'What the Jiminy Cricket was that?' she wanted to know.

'Could have been a jet fighter aircraft,' I surmised.

'My dear man,' she said, 'sorry, I've forgotten your name. You have to forgive me. But what on earth is a "jet"? I know you're not a hundred per cent, but don't go spreading these infernal rumors. Martians maybe? Are we just a little paranoid being woken up in the small hours? Why don't you toddle off back to bed and breathe deeply. If there's one thing I don't want it's a panic. There are people here who could run amok if fear gets hold of them. You have to remember, we have some fully-fledged murderers in here – it's not just a bunch of entertaining wackos.'

I could make no headway, but I knew there were uneasy furtive souls in the Retreat who might be killers just waiting

for their scene. A little later I found myself with David Bone –
he was replacing the tennis rackets that had collapsed out of a
closet with the slipstream of the rush.

He looked up to take a break. 'Now, if I had to imagine the
sound of being buzzed by a pterodactyl – that would be it.'

'Aren't they extinct?' I was sure they were.

'Aha! That's what Challenger and Summerlee thought, isn't
it? Until they met the evidence of their own eyes.'

I breathed deeply; I was upset. 'Pterodactyls in Connecticut?'
I repeated.

Bone grinned – he had an endearing, cheeky smile. 'Nifty
title, that,' he said. 'Make a note of it.'

'I suspect it was a high-speed drone,' I decided. 'We may be
coming under attack.'

'Drone?' said Bone. 'Sounds like bagpipes or snoring.' He
chuckled. 'Pretty deadly combination.'

'You might as well know,' I said. I was speaking quietly so
as not to get over-excited. I felt I had to share the intelligence,
man-to-man. 'A drone is a flying craft, unmanned, sometimes
for observation, but capable of delivering weapon systems. We
have used them in Afghanistan and there is talk of employing
them domestically as sophisticated surveillance.'

'Af-ghanis-tan! My word!' said Bone. 'You really have got it,
haven't you, the works?' He looked at me in the spirit of some
robust skipper resolved not to panic at the hysteria of his crew.
'Afghanistan? Gunga Din country? Why would anyone need
to go there?

'Afghanistan is no laughing matter,' I pointed out. I was
going to say seventeen years and counting. But what was the
point with a 1941 man?

'Stop pulling my leg,' he begged, for the doctor was laughing
so much that he was hardly a suitable authority figure in a state
that yearned for official reassurance.

'Oh, Doctor,' called a voice. Delirium was mounting. It came from a fellow weak at the knees but loping past us, and bearing the weight of a heavy black scab on his upper lip. 'I'll have you know, doc, I am feeling so fragile I should be in bed with a nurse.'

It seemed to be a routine these two had, for Bone shouted back, 'Which nurse do you want?'

'I'm not choosy,' he called out before disappearing. 'Any nurse is nice.'

'There he goes,' said Bone as this bizarre figure vanished. 'Classic case. Anything you say to him, he turns it into a wisecrack. Crazies say the funniest things. Of course, I don't say that in a disparaging way. Just a manner of speaking. But the fact is so many of them have the *sang-froid* of head waiters or butlers from royal households. Have you met Godfrey, by the way? Now there's an example, you'd think he was the rules official at some ancient golf club.'

'I do know Godfrey,' I said. 'Is there anything wrong with him?'

'He thinks he's really from the 500 block on Park Avenue. Distinguished family, Skull and Bones, horses in Virginia, Angus cattle in Maryland, acreage in Delaware. An apartment off the Champs Élysées. A few ex-wives. But here he is, confined in Connecticut. He's actually a bum, off the streets, doesn't have a sou or a soul in the world.'

I could not sleep after this. So I settled in an armchair in the lobby and noticed several newspapers on the table. It looked as if some bored people waiting there had been through them. This irked me; I felt a need to scream. But if you scream in public, people jump to all the worst conclusions about you. Still, I do prefer a pristine folded paper, unopened, a virgin of unexpected stories. I picked up a copy of the *Times*. It was from April 1939 and it reported the very hot Sunday on which the

New York World's Fair had opened. Over 200,000 people were there for the day and there was much interest in a time capsule sealed for the future. Among the many things put inside the capsule was a copy of *Life* magazine, a kewpie doll, writings from Albert Einstein and Thomas Mann, a Mickey Mouse watch, a Gillette safety razor, a packet of Camel cigarettes. The capsule was buried and it was not to be opened until 6939!

I started thinking of what to put in a capsule now – a smart phone, a bullet, an Oculus, a vial of oxycontin, a book by James Salter and another by Stephenie Meyer, a lock of hair each from Caitlyn Jenner and Donald Trump, and why not one of those implants that does the writing for us? The game reminded me of I Packed My Grandmother's Suitcase, which seems such a childish game at first, but then unfailingly reveals every player. You can try it.

Then at dawn, the dawn after the plane flew over us, we were attacked by a trio of fighters, prop planes, circa 1940, I suppose (this is not my field). I was admiring the enthusiasm with which a few people in the garden flung themselves aside, as a signal that they had been hit. In addition, gouts of grass and earth jumped up in the air, like spouts, where the strafing shells dropped. There was blood, too, quite convincing at a distance, and cries of pain and distress. You know the kind of thing. But as if it was a movie that I was watching, I felt confident that nothing was going to hit me. Was that my illness, my lack of reality? Or was I really the star?

'We'd better deal with those bodies.' It was Godfrey. He had his shirtsleeves rolled up and he wore one of those long black aprons you used to see on servants when they were cleaning shoes or wringing a chicken's neck.

I helped him. He knew what to do, and he admitted he had once served in the Ambulance Corps. 'That was a fine mess,' he said. '1915. You wouldn't believe it. The way men were wounded from artillery and shrapnel and then the machine-gun fire that flayed them to shreds. And some of those wrecks would make jokes before they died. Lovely forlorn humor. Everything has been a mess since then. Are you coming to the shore?'

'What for?' I asked. The suggestion startled me, but I smelled adventure and comradeship. The great storm had left a raw stink of ocean in the air. He looked at me, man-to-man, as if the bitter truth had to be admitted.

'Apparently it's dicey over there,' said Godfrey, in the way of a British officer on the line, one who had seen bad stuff but didn't care to let his feelings show or have morale falter.

'The war?' I wondered. Sometimes there are too many catastrophes to choose from.

'And the flooding,' said Godfrey in a gruff way. 'Sully's there already, doing his bit. He asked if you were coming. Said he hoped to see you.'

'Sully?' I realized. 'I *would* like to see him again. He is a fine man.'

But I was hesitant with Godfrey. There was something else I needed to ask, absurd yet essential.

'Do you think we might take Cornelia?' I asked.

He looked at me for what seemed so long I couldn't believe he was without an answer. Not as experienced a man as Godfrey. This must be his close-up! 'You think she could handle it?' he asked. I felt the cross-cut coming back to me. We were connected!

'It'll be hard?' I said.

'Bound to be. No picnic.'

'I think she's…'

He smiled. 'What? What do you think, old chap?'

'The harder the better,' I decided. 'I would like to ask her.'

'Done and done. Why didn't you say? It may be terrible out there, terrible beyond our grasp, but female company can be better than breakfast. And she's tougher than she knows.' So said this brave butler, at the dawn of the Second World War.

'Then we should go,' I said, I know I said it. 'After all, my friend, we are the Connecticuts.'

'Pop goes the weasel,' said Godfrey, like crossing his fingers.

* * *

Associated Press, 28 December 2012. The death of Fontella Bass is reported. She had died where she was born, in St Louis. She was seventy-two and she had had several strokes in her last years. She was best known for her 1965 hit song, 'Rescue Me'.

Some songs reach out and claim you – you're mad about them, you say. 1965 was before the best or the worst: Vietnam would get so much worse, and the demon of liberation was yet to find its seductive dance. My own life then felt calm and sure, though I daresay some companions would have laughed at that estimate. I had never heard of Fontella Bass, but I heard the demanding beat and the writhing, coiling height of her song, like a child's voice in the crowd and tumult, calling for you. So it is a song of losing hope as much as yearning for it, and I heard that conflict in Fontella Bass's voice though I had never heard of her. She was speaking to me.

There is an interview with Ms Bass on YouTube, done only a few years before her death, in which she says, well, of course, it's a love song, but it's political too. The rescue the singer wants touches on the condition of black people in St Louis and elsewhere and in Vietnam, too, where that tragedy was taking shape. There was an age in which every love song was political, and it may be the fusion that makes young experience so heady. I knew in a vague yet certain way that the simple call, 'Rescue Me', was both my need and the energy that would destroy me. Yes, it was only a pop song, with Fontella Bass in

a weird mod suit and a hat while the white gang – the birds
– of *Ready, Steady, Go*, danced behind her. It was the system,
selling records, when a small black disc was like the satin heart
in Valentine cards.

Bass herself was not rescued. The song was a hit, but Chess
Records, who released it, managed to pay her very little, despite
her being a co-writer on the song. Years later, the recording was
used in an American Express ad, without Bass's knowledge,
and she was successful in suing for $50,000.

'Rescue Me!' – Why? Are you in prison? The other day I was
on a radio show, talking about the movies, and a caller said,
Well, he went to the movies for escape, and didn't really like
to think about them too much. Me, too, I said, and all of us.
Since they began, the movies have been a way of escaping a life
that might be disappointing. But then I said maybe sometimes
we owed it to ourselves to ask what it was we were escaping
from, and why. 'Rescue Me' poses those questions, and offers
the bitter-sweet hope that love may do it.

Of course, I'm mad, I know it now, and I can cope with
it. That is what Connecticut is for. But I miss the comfort I
grew up with that the others, the rest of the world, the other
wounded, might be sane.

EIGHT

This chapter is not easily believed. You might dismiss it because of rumors of unsoundness in your author. You may want to say 'our' Connecticut could not be like this. But I am telling you what I saw, and you should know that 'your' Connecticut belongs to a lot of other people. There are things in the world that should not happen, but that has not prevented them. There's a hole in the world and we're falling in.

Dogs gnawing babies; crows pecking at the spent eyes; children poking the corpses of other children to see if anything might be a means of trade. Cornelia howling, and Godfrey glancing at me to see if we should press on. Deep, wide ruts left by the bulldozers and the military vehicles, some of them filled up with these dead bodies. The clothes they wore – summer frocks and bright shirts – were pressed into the flesh by the tread of the vehicles. Cornelia was walking with her eyes closed. So many of us are sleepwalkers. There is ceaseless industry in getting rid of the bodies.

We hardly guessed what going towards the shore entailed. In the first few miles, there was damage from the storm: the limbs of trees tossed aside, entire growth ripped up at the white roots, glaring in the sun. It was a fine day – the weather had no tact. Then came the war zone, a layer cake of slaughter. There were tanks and huge artillery pieces firing into the distance.

'Those shells must carry several miles,' said Godfrey. 'Never seen anything like them before.'

'What would they be firing at?' asked Cornelia. There was no reason for an answer. Heavier guns than these have been aimed at us all our lives and no one discusses them.

There were pits where the people who had dug out the hole were then pushed down into the ground and shot by waiting troops. Then a pause and officers with pistols searching for movement among the dead or dying. I wondered if some of those victims might be feigning death – you hear of such things. But the next step was for gasoline to be hosed into the pit and ignited. The flames billowed up from below the surface of the earth, as if its fire was breaking free. And Sully was nowhere to be found. In view of what was going on we were glad he was not there, and fearful of looking beneath a helmet's steel brim and finding his tanned smile. Would he still smile at this? There were soldiers joking and laughing at the odd shapes the corpses took. It is a wonder what can be amusing.

'What is this for?' I asked one of the executioners, nodding at the bizarre death-piles.

'Reprisals, that's what for,' he told me, and gave me a wink as if at one unkind word Godfrey and I might be helping to fill up some pit. Then he noticed Cornelia and became more dangerous on the spot. 'You should see the things they done to our boys.' He said it to her, for her.

'Who were they?' asked Godfrey.

'Resistance?' was the answer. 'Rebels. Traitors. Scum. Naughty boys.' And then another wink. 'It's orders, isn't it? I like your lady. Nice bit of stuff.'

'That's right,' said another soldier, though his uniform seemed to come from a different army. 'They shut hundreds of our lads in a church and just threw bombs into it. They're not human. If I had ten minutes, dear, I'd give you the shock you deserve.' He reached a rough hand towards her, and she recoiled as if it was cholera.

The first soldier was looking at the pit and its roast. 'There's meat down there, my son,' he told his chum. 'In famine, don't you see, you get to eat the enemy – the only way – though personally I do find the aftertaste of gasoline upsetting. Gives me the runs. I would prefer a nice gravy like mother used to make. Do you make gravy, darling?' he asked Cornelia.

'No,' hissed Cornelia, the sound slipping through her teeth. When I looked at her I saw how constant fear can release a need for revenge. 'I can't stand it,' she said. I was afraid her anger might arouse these men. Nearly my lover at last, she might be ready to murder everyone – or get us killed. But these soldiers were subdued for a moment by her Park Avenue authority. You can bully a trained man with a firm voice. Then she seized the sidearm from one of them – he gave it up as a gift – and one-two, seventy-five and seventy-six, she shot them both in the head. Their eyes popped in blood and oblivion. They fell like trees.

'Now you've done it!' I told her. Yet no one noticed. With enough killing in the air, the general attitude becomes absent-minded, or not inclined to keep count.

'Hush, child,' I said and put my arms around Cornelia. I wanted the gesture to mean so much. It didn't do a thing. She was her own empty anger, hollowed out and toxic, like the shell of a reactor at a deserted power station. Her gun dropped in the mud like fresh shit.

'Settle down, old fellow.' It was Godfrey at my shoulder. I felt from his tone that he might have a brandy for me on a silver tray, a comforter, but he was actually holding the ruined arm of a child. Something he had found on the battlefield. I guessed it came from a girl around ten (to judge from the fingers and their chipped pink nail polish) but there was a tattoo on the arm, a snake writhing around the muscle and ready to bite at the wrist. It was colored green and mauve and the violent design made me nervous. But there was only the arm to behold.

'Found it propped against a tree,' said Godfrey. 'As if someone thought the owner might come back looking for it.'

The sky, white like dead flesh, lined and scarred but not yet hinged, seamed or diminished.

* * *

'Hi, I'm governor of Connecticut and I just want to say don't be strangers. I know, you've heard the stories about our state being the national home for loonies. That's put you off. OK – learn some facts. We *are* the nation's depositing place for disturbed people, but that means money for the state, Uncle Sam money that has gone into hotels, restaurants, spas, golf courses, try-your-luck casinos, the list goes on. And 93.1 per cent of our new citizens are not just harmless, they're friendly, educated, without political or religious affiliations, and many of them have amazing stories and useful lives, as well as grant support. Then there's the photo opportunity to impress your friends. Crazy people a lot of the time do funny things and this is a candid camera state. You want to know more, go to comeondownconnecticut.org and say the governor sent you.'

* * *

'Now, Miss Vasco da Gama, you are from the Dominican Republic?'

'That is what he liked to say.'

'He invented it?'

'He makes stuff up.'

'You are not from Hispaniola?'

'Make it Bakersfield.'

'That's very interesting. He got many things wrong?'

'Until he was right.'

'But you were a dancer?'

'I liked to shake it out.'

'And your papers are all in order?'

'Pop goes the weasel. He used to say that.'

'Indeed. And you were researching scenes from movies that involved kissing?'

'Sort of thing.'

'He was a scholar of osculatory coincidence?'

'Is that smooching?'

'Just so. Were you by chance ever up a country lane at night kissing him?'

'Never left the library.'

'Now, presumably, Miss Vasco da Gama, this kissing might sometimes go further?'

'Not that I noticed. It was the kissing he wanted. He was like an old-timer panning for gold, like anyone looking for a lost car key. Sort of thing.'

* * *

During that break, Cornelia had been pressing my hand like a stroke victim using a last means of contact (or was she squeezing an endless trigger?)... and who had come along out of the marshland on the flood that was seeping in from the shore, but dear old Sully.

He stood, swaying in a battered blue punt, poling his way towards us. He was leaner than I remembered him. He seemed older. But that cheery grin had lost nothing. He was Sully, our stalwart. 'Ahoy, skipper,' he called to me, and let the pole slip through his hands to find a muddy shore.

Godfrey came back to me to report. 'Old chap, the consensus

is that everyone's got the grim point. This is an ugly scene, like all the bad stuff we have known from other, less fortunate histories.'

'You said it!' I cried; I was carried away with disasterism, feverish for mayhem. 'I am about to describe the devastation from the hurricane at the shore. Look at Sully. Has he got stories to tell?'

'I know, I know,' said Godfrey in a soothing way. 'But the governor says hurricanes hardly happen, so look on the bright side. I daresay that opinion's iffy, strictly as science, but in the short term a calming message serves a useful purpose. Maybe you have a few jokes you could share? Some brisk repartee? You wouldn't guess the fracas I've averted in my time just by announcing cocktails.'

'Oh, yes,' said Cornelia, 'a calming message – let it be that. And perhaps one small drinky?'

'I have pages of famine, murder and destruction to do still,' I told her – I was worked up; I yearned for respect and pitiless splendor. Was I to be censored?

'That is only going to upset people,' said Cornelia. 'It will upset you, too. You know it will.' I had an inkling she might have been talking to the editor.

I told Cornelia, 'I thought you had a steel edge to match the beauty of your gaze and your killing certainty.' (I did say that, but I admit I'm not happy with the line – rewrite?)

'Oh, how sweet,' she answered in a preoccupied way. 'I sometimes wish I could do the other with you, I do, I really do. But tell us a nice story, won't you?'

Sully chimed in. 'You know, pal, this is exactly the fix I got in doing movies. When times get hard enough, there's a limit to reminding people, rubbing their noses in it. They're longing for a little fun.'

'Plus I do think we've got this message by now,' said Godfrey. 'We can imagine the unimaginable, so long as we can be spared the actual.' He paused, and then, 'But, look, over there, do you see what I see?' His eyes and his voice widened – his optimism soared. 'A little girl with just one arm!' Godfrey was cheering up by the second. 'Now, wouldn't she make a heartwarming episode done right?'

'She's adorable,' said Cornelia. 'It could be a part for Shirley Temple.'

Well, as you can imagine, the gap between this torn waif coming our way and the celebrated and house-trained Ms Temple was as far as that between the beach at Cabo San Lucas and the one at Fukushima.

The child seemed ten, maybe elevenish. Her dress was dirty and torn, and the shabby gray blondeness of her matted hair was like her face. One arm, the left, was gone, just above the elbow, but the ragged stump seemed to have dried. I think someone had had the presence of mind to dip it in hot tar.

The child had stopped a little way off and was examining us with destroyed eyes, trying to decide whether we were friendly or treacherous. Fear had scraped her life force away. Whenever we have one of our shooting outrages you are likely to see a kid's face – victim or perpetrator, it's all the same – cut off from hope or surprise. We beckoned to her but she would not come close.

Sully settled the matter. He had his swag bag on his back. He swung it down, delved inside, and asked, 'Chocolate?'

The child ignored this but, 'Oh, perfect,' said Cornelia, 'I'd love some choccy.' Amid tumult and disaster, she could not ignore her sweet tooth, or the thought of a treat.

'What happened with your arm?' Godfrey asked the child.

'Came off,' she said. 'Came off in the war.'

'Is that it over there?' wondered Godfrey with a discreet nod. A training in service can prepare someone to ask the most awkward questions.

And so we beheld a child surveying her own severed arm. She examined it; it was hers. But the arm seemed like lies she had told once, intimate and incriminating. Godfrey said to me, 'If we can get her to a hospital, it might be reattached.'

But the girl said, 'No. I don't like that arm. I wanted to take it off. Some guys did the tat on it last year.' She stood looking at the arm as if it was a snapshot from embarrassing childhood. She was not touched by nostalgia. So we buried the arm, and in that plain of mud I doubt any of us could find it again.

'What's your name?' Cornelia asked the girl. Was there a note of the maternal in her voice?

'Don't remember,' said our new acquaintance. She said it with a dull ferocity that suggested her memory had been extracted.

'Are you a forgotten girl?' asked Godfrey. 'I'm a forgotten man, you know, or I was. Think of a name for us.'

This may have been the first test in the girl's life other than the task of surviving. Was she ready to pick a number and have it inscribed on her last arm? 'I don't know,' she said. 'Are you queer or something? What about Susan?'

'There's a Susan in the book already,' I had to admit – I wanted to disappear.

'Fuck that,' said the girl. 'What about "Unique"? You got a Unique?'

'As a name?' asked Cornelia. She was daunted by the tenacity of the child, and such resolve in a broken body.

The girl went into a list – were these lost friends? You couldn't tell from her flattened recitation. 'Alexandra, Alice, Albertine, Allison, Angela, Anna, Anne, Arlene…'

'Unique will do fine,' decided Godfrey, cutting off her catalogue. 'And I'm Godfrey.'

'Fuck that, too,' said the girl. All of which is building towards the point – and I might as well tell you now – that what we ended up calling her was 'Fuck That', until one day (I mustn't

DAVID THOMSON   123

jump too far ahead) I saw a proud wrinkle of smile on her
lowered face at its use. But she saw me looking, strode up to me
and said… well, you can surmise what she said.

NINE

We then experienced a transformation, enough to suggest you never can tell. As we hurried away from the damage of war, expecting a rough march of many days to reach a more tolerable world, it took only an hour to be restored to the soft folds of tranquil Connecticut. There was no terrorist fence to keep the riffraff out. There was not a hint of a no man's land, minefields or poisoned no-go acres, and no wall to signal Connecticut's safety. We observed no fiscal cliff or slough of despond. The winter light of disaster gave way to the balm of a summer afternoon in the countryside. The wasteland became a gladed meadow with woods on the hillside as if put there by Monet.

'Stop this glop!' said Fuck That.

Birds sang and scents circled in the shade under the trees, grinding the hot air. 'Oh, that's better,' sighed Cornelia, and she took off her battle-scarred Mainbocher jacket to enjoy the warmth. In the sun, her sleeveless silk shirt (early Edith Head or late Travis Banton) seemed flimsier than ever. The outline of her breasts might have been drawn in by Matisse as two quick scoops. She was beautiful again and she smiled aimlessly at me, as if it was a natural thing to be. Even Fuck That felt the shift.

The child had been studying the details of the landscape – the trees, the birds, the peace – as if they might have been elements in a trap. As she walked along, she was looking for people tracking us or for signs of sinister enterprise in what you might call the décor. Once she whirled round so suddenly that she lost her footing and fell over. I realized she was not yet skilled at balancing her lost arm. She was angered by the fall, and snarled when I sought to help her.

'Don't you see,' she said. 'It's too quiet to be natural. We're walking into an ambush.'

'Have you not known countryside before?' I asked. I began to realize that she was conditioned by broken buildings, streets beyond repair and human figures somewhere between vagrancy and savagery.

'I seen movies about them woods,' she said, 'with rapists and killers and loonies waiting there.'

'Those are just stories,' I said. 'As it happens, my child, you are walking along with three of your so-called "loonies" all sent to Connecticut for rest and calm.'

She looked at me as if she now saw that I could be unsound, and it disconcerted her that a 'loony' was still doing his best to be a citizen, to the point of rescuing her, or bringing a little comfort.

'All three of you?' she demanded. 'I could tell she was crackers.' Cornelia was up ahead, her hand trailing in the long grasses beside the path.

'How so?' I asked. I wanted to hear this child's opinion on Cornelia.

''Cause she's such a looker,' said Fuck That. 'Never met a looker who wasn't bad news.'

'But her looks are natural,' I said. 'Some people simply are... well, what we call beautiful. It can't be helped.'

'Am I?' It was as if a sudden rat had poked its mouth into mine and bitten me.

I longed for a deft author to write an escape for me. 'Not at first sight perhaps,' I faltered. 'You need a bath, a comfortable bed, a square meal, a trust fund, a comb for your hair –'

'And pretty flowers where my arm is gone?' she sneered.

'You are abused and unfortunate,' I told her. 'Those things don't guarantee the absence of beauty.'

'Shit they don't!' she said. 'You say that. You'd make speeches about that. But you don't live by it. You believe good-looking is good, sucker. That's why you're hot for cold Corny.'

'That's a fair point,' I admitted. 'But if you learn to look at anyone long enough you will see good.' I sounded like Lillian Gish!

She laughed, but without a smile. 'You are nuts,' she said. 'You look at that Cornelia long enough you'll get the chill in her eyes, the gin on her breath and how she can't be trusted. You're seeing money. It's always the same.'

We walked along in silence for several minutes. I could not refute her bleak case. And then she said, 'So, you're dead sure we're not being followed?'

'I'm certain,' I said.

'Well, if we're not being followed, Hawkeye, what's that leopard keeps coming after us?'

We stopped and she pointed with her good arm. At first I couldn't see it – I suppose life had not trained me to notice the tiny signs of activity that a good scout picks up. But then I saw a slither of amber in the sunlight. A few seconds later, there was what could only be a leopard, not so much furtive as unhappy, low to the ground, slinking along, more ashamed than malicious. 'That's Baby,' I realized. 'He just wants to be with us.'

'Wants to eat us,' said Fuck That. 'That's what he wants.'

But once we halted, Baby came up to us, more quickly and gratefully. Of course, he was disappointed that we had nothing to offer him, but he seemed incapable of eating us instead.

I had an idea, so I said to Fuck That, 'Perhaps you would like to look after Baby. He seems good-natured and fun to stroke. He would be company for you, a kind of pet.'

She looked at me in something close to disgust. 'That would be cutty,' she said.

Though Fuck That gave little evidence of taking care of anything, Baby joined us in the low-slung stride and padding step that all who know leopards will cherish. In half an hour, when Baby paused to sniff a wild flower, Fuck That did look over her shoulder (the armless one) and growl, 'C'm'n', whereupon the meek beast fell in step and came close enough to Fuck That's bare leg for a damp whisker to make contact. I could have swooned when the surly child said, 'Cut that out', in a tone only likely to have a pushy boy think of more than a snatched kiss.

I ambled along, and nearly bumped into a speechless Cornelia. She had stopped in her tracks and had her arms outstretched so that a sudden gathering of small blue butterflies could rest on her. I don't know where they had come from, but several hundred of these delicate insects – none more than an inch and a half from one wingtip to the other – had alighted on the white sleeves of that shirt, on her head and face, on her shoulders and on her chest. She might have been nervous, but I could see from her eyes, as much as the flutter of pale blue wings allowed, that she was ecstatic. She was like an illustration from a fairy story. She kept silent only to avoid the mishap of eating a butterfly.

'I would kiss you,' I said, 'but I can't.'

At which, without any other movement, Cornelia very carefully pursed her lips and blew outwards. It was a puff, not strong enough to blow out a candle, but several of the blues were lifted up on the gentle draft. They fluttered from her mouth like bubbles in champagne. I leaned forward and kissed her. There, I did it, without disturbing any other of the blues.

When our mouths parted again, she said so that only I could hear, 'You must call me Lilith now.' Something was liberated in her. She had been traded! To another mental health clinic. Chestnut Lodge. Just as I had her, she was removed.

I remonstrated with Dr Bone. He was sheepish. 'Management,' he muttered. 'I had no part in it. Some salary cap issue.'

I saw Cornelia waving at me with a wistful smile for her new life.

TEN

By now, it may be clear that the affect and mood of a modest estate in the country on a calm summer evening is just about the epitome of Connecticut. So imagine such an occasion, with human figures as emblems of romance – or not. When Cornelia recognized that she had become Lilith it was like… well, let's say it was like Norman becoming Mother. A gamechanger.

'Lilith, there you are,' said a young man, dark, painfully handsome but tense enough to crack. 'We couldn't find you anywhere. Dr Brice was terribly concerned. She told me to search for you.'

'I was here, Vincent.' It was Cornelia answering, and in a lower or more seductive voice than I was used to – it was Lilith's voice. 'I was always here. I saw you searching.' He became markedly more insecure to think that she had observed his uneasiness.

In becoming Lilith, in taking on that brazen and mythic persona, Cornelia had been traded to a new asylum or storyline, with fresh people in charge of her. And she flirted with this Vincent so that he hunched and seemed to sink into his own shoulders in doubt and desire. She appeared to be at home here. Carved in stone above the double doorway to this new building was its name, 'Chestnut Lodge'. There was ivy growing on the walls and wisteria planted next to them. Now 'Lilith' grew there too, as pretty as lilies, but deadly nightshade.

'What did you do to your clothes?' Vincent chided her. He sounded shocked, but Cornelia or Lilith answered casually, 'Oh, we were in the war, you know.'

'How is the war?' asked Vincent. He was a boy, bewildered, or fearful. He made the hostilities sound like an elderly and infirm relative.

'Quite horrid,' she told him. And then she sidled up to me, and whispered, 'He's crazy about me, can you tell? And he's supposed to be my nurse!'

Why was I surprised? We had stumbled upon another clinic in another secluded spot. If Connecticut took in all the nervous and disturbed cases from everywhere surely it must need many similar establishments to The Retreat. So was it surprising that Cornelia might have a sudden fresh allegiance? An actress may play Electra and do Electrolux commercials in the same day.

But I soon appreciated the contrast between Chestnut Lodge and the Bone clinic. Dr Brice turned out to be hushed, learned and iron. David Bone was chatty, confused and like a favorite comforter. Whereas he and Susan Bone seemed to assume that mental illness or rarity was everywhere, so why bother to disguise that, Dr Brice prowled her empire as a guardian of repression and regularity. She was a handsome, middle-aged woman who gave every sign of having dieted in a flagellating manner. Her clothes were expensive yet self-denying. She was steadily polite without ever concealing her totalitarian attitude. So at Chestnut Lodge the custodians were dedicated to stifling eccentricity or misbehavior, determined that no draft or chill ever entered the building. Dr Brice let it be known that order would prevail. (Secretly, she was designing uniforms for her nurses.) Dr Bone never harbored any such hope. He was easy-going with every vagary, especially his own. Dr Brice had a horror of her mistakes. I saw her once break down in fury because she had misused the word 'disinterest' – a very human failing.

This all encouraged Dr Brice's fear that she might be a victim of conspiracy. Vincent, the nurse, was especially prey to that atmosphere. He seemed a likeable loner or outcast, but Brice was making an agonized policeman of him, and Lilith (or Cornelia 2) was a meticulous exploiter of his indecision. Her new, flagrant, Irene-ish manner was designed to break him down.

'I fucked Vincent last night – you see, I really can do it, it's like riding a bicycle – and then I called him "Vinny" in front of Brice. He started to panic and Brice had to order him to the Quiet Room to rest.'

One afternoon, walking in the garden (but keeping off the grass), I raised the subject of the Bones with Dr Brice. Oh yes, she knew of them; they had met at conferences, but…, 'Well, I find the wife a strain.'

'You know, I don't believe they are married.'

Her eyebrows rose, like a push-up. 'That makes matters worse.' She was more confirmed than surprised.

'They are afraid of divorce,' I tried to explain.

'Isn't she just a touch unsteady?'

'Without doubt,' I said. 'But that's her charm.'

'Hmm. I had a professor once who said there was no such thing as charm. It was a highly skilled, chronic behavioral ploy.'

'Were there really professors like that once?' I asked.

'Where did you study?' she wanted to know.

'I haven't studied,' I replied.

'But…' She stopped in our walk so I had to stop, too. 'I beg your pardon. You *are* a doctor?'

'No, I'm a patient.'

'Oh, you had seemed to be the leader of your band – Lilith, the gamine urchin, and that butler type. I assumed you were their care-giver.'

I smiled. I was a little cheered at the mistake. 'No,' I said. 'I was sent to Connecticut, too, not so long ago.'

I suspect she regarded that as a warning sign, or the onset of institutionalization. But her coast was clear now, it was promisingly bare: if I had no credentials, it meant that my patients, including myself, were prizes for her. I did not tell her we would not be staying long enough for any course of treatment. A few meals would be enough. Fuck That was especially devoted to the Chestnut Lodge dining room, and she was eating meat loaf and chocolate pudding there three times a day on the same plate. It was while dining there that we first encountered Spoff.

I heard him first. I was picking over a late lunch when I heard this voice coming from behind an alcove. It sounded like a man well into his seventies, or a corncrake (I'm not sure what that bird sounds like, but I trust its name). He was calling to a waitress, 'I wonder, pretty lady, if there is any more of the artichoke hollandaise.'

'Sure, toots,' she had replied. 'Coming right up.'

There was something so grave in his voice, and such a hint of the gourmand in his request, that I was intrigued. I contrived to knock my napkin ring off our table so that I had to get up to retrieve it. As I rounded the alcove wall, following the ring's roll, searching for an old man, I saw nothing but a small boy perched on two telephone directories so that he could be high enough to eat at the grown-up table. I was perplexed, until the boy noticed me and said, 'Those napkin rings can acquire a life of their own.' It was the voice. And what had been something spellbinding to the ear alone was a phenomenon once one realized that embalmed words were emerging from this unsmiling kid. It was his gravitas that made me think he might be a suitable pal for Fuck That.

His name was Henry Spofford III. How he came to be in Connecticut is a long and unnecessary story, but Dr Brice told me he was an unusual case: though only eleven, he believed that he was seventy-seven, and so he had developed several of the characteristics of that age – a deep and ancient voice, the urge to chat with waitresses and the like, and a steady state of pert melancholy. He took his meals. He sat in the gardens in a deckchair, with a blanket even on the warmest day. He read trashy novels and followed reports of cricket.

'Fuck That!' I realized. I couldn't resist it – I was thinking of our urchin, old beyond her years, who might make an odd affinity with Spoff.

I was there when the two of them met at breakfast. I doubt I have ever seen more incredulity and hostility gathered in so few years. Face-to-face, they tried to deny presence. It was like looking in a mirror and not seeing yourself.

Fuck That broke the ice (looking for a fragment she could employ as a weapon?). 'Henry Spofford the turd?' she said, affecting a south Dublin accent.

The old kid considered, and then after eating an entire chocolate profiterole, and licking the spoon, he said, 'Fuck you, cherub!' They were off. It seemed to onlookers (I discussed this with Godfrey) that they both believed they were with an alien being, despite some deeper admission that this other must have been human once. It was like finding a fossil of yourself.

'What brings you here, my flower?'

'I walked.'

'I was delivered by limousine,' he said, 'a Packard. Pleasant.'

'I was never in a limo.'

'It's no more than a very awkward room made of leather.'

'How do you talk like that, turdy?'

'Well, lover, I just flap my tongue.'

'I'm not your lover.'

'A mere pleasantry, young lady.'

'I'm older than you. You ever seen dead bodies, ankle-deep?'

'Up to my thigh,' said Spofford without a tremor.

'Why are you here, turd?'

'It slips my mind, buttercup.'

'Can you read?'

'Of course – may I read to you some time, honeyed one?'

'Fuck yes!'

'I do not read words like that.'

'It's my new name – Fuck That.'

'Do you have a real name?'

'Susan.'

'Acceptable. Pleasing. I will not allow abbreviations, though. Banish "Susie" or "Sue" from your thoughts.'

'Certainly, Hank.'

'And don't try the acid with me, orphan of the storm.'

* * *

For just a few days, Chestnut Lodge presented itself as a bitter-sweet paradise. With war just over the hill! The sweetness lay in witnessing the developing friendship between Henry Spofford III and Fuck That. The solemnity of the boy and the depravity of the girl coalesced in a way none of us would have thought possible. They could be seen together on the lawn, with him reading to her in his gruff chant, and her responding as if he was Ronald Colman (a star of the 1920s and 30s). Across the lawn, Godfrey and I could hear the splash of her laughter. We were taken aback at first since we had never heard that laugh. This was followed by the foghorn boom of Henry saying, 'Was that a joke I told?' The charm there is in watching young people develop, especially those who had seemed set back in life. The fresh air, a glimpse of nature and simple companionship – the principles of Connecticut, I suppose – are easily mocked by urban sophisticates who like to pass off the tangle of their own lives as an engrossing puzzle or an obscure example of 'modern art'.

It was during this reverie that Lilith came up to me with the panache of conquest. The frigid beauty *sans merci* had changed. Vincent was so led astray by her that Dr Brice was considering having him removed from the Lodge. There was even an occasion when Lilith was working on a loom, weaving a tapestry (the inmates had an array of wholesome pastimes). Vincent was hovering over her as she managed to add her own long hair (this had grown with astonishing but convenient speed) into the fabric of weaving. Trapped in it, her auburn hair fusing with the red and gold silks (hadn't she been a brunette once? I asked Godfrey), she seemed like a witch or a nymph. Vincent was enchanted by the sight. But then, Lilith simply withdrew her head and stood up, leaving a convincing wig as part of the tapestry, like an animal caught there. At once, she resembled the Cornelia who had a cloche of dark hair. She laughed out loud, and left Vincent on his knees as if he was preparing for an amateur production of the life of Toulouse-Lautrec.

She came across the lawn in a kind of dance – Cornelia and Lilith, but who was leading? – and she stopped to look at me. 'You know,' she said in a taunting way, 'I can imagine taking a sentimental walk in the woods with you. Your dream come true? Or did you only desire me so long as joining was impossible? I know that sort. Is that why you're here in Connecticut? You did desire me, didn't you? And I know what longing is like. Wouldn't you say, Godfrey, that I'm just a little wilder now than Irene?'

'Well,' said Godfrey, attempting to serve as peacemaker.

'Or perhaps *you're* more drawn to the woods, Godfrey?' she suggested. 'Don't think your cool butler act ever fooled me.' She turned to me. 'Did you know that our Godfrey has a shameful past? He was a man-about-town once, with a smart wife and a darling dog. But Godfrey drank to distraction, and one day he was arrested for beating the dog. Nearly killed the poor thing. Did I miss anything, Godfrey?'

My friend was silent, his face covered in gloom and thunder. 'You are always right, Cornelia,' he said. 'It is your curse. No one can stand such correctness for company.'

This seemed to sting her, for she turned on the spot and was about to thrash a few flowers for sport, when we all heard the sound of a small plane. It did not seem well.

It was a biplane, and it was wavering just as it showed an intermittent dipping motion that was helpless, but disturbing. Was it dreaming of landing on the Lodge lawn? The ornate, if not clunky, stone bird bath and sundial in its center was not an encouragement.

'That's Irene's plane,' cried Cornelia, more with interest than alarm. 'She's come to visit.'

'I believe she's in trouble,' said Godfrey. 'Losing height, dropping speed.'

'Not to worry,' said Cornelia. 'It's a De Havilland. One wing's called Joanie and the other Livia.' But then she cried out, 'Oh!'

You would need a recording to convey the sudden pitch of horror in Cornelia's voice. 'Oh!', even with an exclamation mark, is poor value. But it's what she said, and I am not prepared to play fast and loose with fact at a moment as delicate as this. The plane had pitched forward as if a weight had shifted to its nose, and thus it plunged to the ground, though it contrived to coincide with the base of an ancient oak tree because of a last-minute zig in mid-air, like a girl tossing her hair when she thinks to be noticed.

The tree was scarred and gouged, but the cockpitted Irene (she might have smiled) was expiring. We removed her leather helmet and a pair of goggles, only to discover that her head had an unconventional wobble to it. 'I never can find that bloody Howland Island,' she breathed, and those would have been her last words (some slipshod biographies do have them as that), but in fact I had the presence of mind to strap my watch on her empty wrist, so that, 'Sweetie!', was the very last utterance from this unimpeded sensualist, certain she was late. I hardly needed the watch myself.

I remember that Godfrey was in tears. Cornelia spoke in a whisper, 'So now I'm sole heir to the Bullock millions. No reason to deny it.'

'Really?' said Dr Brice, dreaming of an endowment.

* * *

Carole Lombard died in a plane crash on 16 January 1942, at about 7.30pm local time. It was dark by then. She was returning from Indianapolis, her home town, where she had played a leading part in a war bonds drive that raised over $2 million. She was traveling with her mother, Bess Peters, and Otto Winkler, who was press agent to her husband, Clark Gable.

The Transcontinental and Western Air DC-3 landed at the old Las Vegas airport, Alamo Field, for refueling and then headed south-west on its way to Burbank. It was a clear night with what were described as ideal flying conditions. But the plane crashed into a cliff face on Potosi Mountain about thirty-two miles south-west of Las Vegas. All twenty-two people on board were killed in the explosion that occurred. Lombard was thirty-three, a flame in a fireball

* * *

'How could a pretty lady die that way?' asked Henry Spofford III.

'In the war,' said Fuck That, 'the planes came down like leaves.'

There was anguish in her voice, I thought. It often comes with fondness. There is no vulnerability like it, not even living in a city being bombed or waiting for the sound of boots on the stairs.

'Everybody inside,' said Dr Brice. 'I'll have this all cleaned up.' Her hand waved at the wrecked plane and the broken Irene. 'We might donate the plane to a local school. Don't you think it would be interesting for them?'

The next day, without fuss or parents, the madcap was buried in a far corner of the Chestnut Lodge gardens – I noticed a platoon of other graves, sinking into the soft ground. There was only the memorial the few of us put together. Cornelia spoke impromptu, incoherent, ravaged that her essential opponent was gone. I noticed that she slipped a fine watch on her sister's left wrist – I wonder if it worked. (It was companion to the watch I had given her at the time of the crash.)

Godfrey read a nice passage from *Gentlemen Prefer Blondes* and I – well, I was of a mind at first to read something modern, but the Lodge library stopped at 1940, so I offered the conclusion to *The Great Gatsby*, because I have found that it covers most American occasions. Henry Spofford III and Fuck That stood side by side with wild flowers clutched in their hands. They were so close now that they apparently forgot they had not known Irene until seconds after her neck snapped. Funerals bring people together in a way weddings seldom manage.

When it was over, Fuck That came up to me, wide-eyed and contrite and said, 'I would like you to call me Susan from now on'. I surveyed her for a moment without a smear of expression, and, of course, I told her, 'Fuck that'. And that one-armed brat laughed wildly, stamped her foot and threw her flowers at me, the stems hot from her hand.

Our Susan.

ELEVEN

So, my being brought to Connecticut had prompted a lot of activity, not all of it pleasant, but action has a way of erasing melancholy. Researching and writing *The Kiss in Movies* (or *Smooching the Screen*, I was torn over the title) had made little impression on either the world, or me. But now, I had friends, people I knew: Godfrey, Sully (wherever he was), as well as two misbegotten children to look after, not to mention David and Susan Bone.

Sooner or later, most people who tend the mentally disturbed need some help themselves. I was sorry that my quest for a romantic-sexual-conversational pal in Cornelia was frustrated again. But I believed by then that I had only begun to write out of the hope of creating people I liked as companions.

After Irene's funeral, I felt an urge to move on and get back to 'my' place, the Bone clinic, a haven where I had my appointments. Godfrey was similarly inclined and he suggested that we might as well leave Cornelia at Chestnut to settle who she was. Watching her could only fuel her melodrama. But we did not wish to entrust Henry Spofford III and Fuck That to the untender regime of Dr Brice. Both kids were in flux, emerging from a kind of prison, and Godfrey and I would not shrug off our roles of guardian, or onlooker. We wanted to care for them, and we were eager to see what would happen to them. For all we knew, Spofford III was on his way to founding a religion, while Fuck That might be the heretic to bring that same church down in scandal. We agreed to take the children with us.

We imagined we must be a long way from the Bones, and we were concerned about how far we could expect the children to walk. But Connecticut is a small world when it wants to be, and we went on only a little over an hour with Fuck That singing songs that seemed to pass over Spofford's head, and leave Godfrey bewildered. He was still wearing tails and a white tie, you understand, in case on our journey the need for butler business might arise.

So we came over a ridge heavy with lupin and cow parsley, to see the Bone clinic only a mile away, as happy as an orchard in the sunlight. This gave me a sense of Connecticut being like the terrain of Fenimore Cooper, with a few forts in the forest, and Magua and Hawkeye leaping through the undergrowth. (If you haven't tried Connecticut, you should. I realize parts of this narrative may be off-putting, but it's only a story and Connecticut is a holiday.)

What should we see, as we came down the slope, but David and Susan Bone playing croquet on the lawn. David appeared to be losing, perhaps because he was allowing Susan to cheat or had too little knowledge of the rules to notice it. But on seeing us, he happily gave up the game and came towards me, waving his mallet like a flag of welcome.

'Didn't know where you'd got to,' he said in that cheerful yet desperate way he maintained. 'Knew you'd turn up. Who are the nippers?'

I introduced them and Bone immediately did a handstand to amuse them. Fuck That treated the performance with disdain, but Spofford III bent over at the waist so that he could continue to look David in the eye. Henry was an upright fellow even in that pose, but when he offered to shake hands with David, and that good sport offered his own hand in return, that is how the handstand collapsed, in a cascade of Bone laughter.

I next had to break the news about the Bullock girls to Dr Bone: how Cornelia had remained at Chestnut Lodge, while Irene had left the problems of her mind behind.

'No!' cried Bone. 'She was making progress, wasn't she? How did she do it?'

'Drowned, I bet,' said Susan with authority, 'like Virginia Woolf in the Ouse.' (28 March 1941.)

'Not at all,' I said. 'She was flying a plane and it crashed.'

'Had to give it a spin,' surmised David. 'Well, that tears our game, Susan. I must do the paperwork on her. Worst part of this job.'

'Exactly our sentiments on the Western Front,' said Godfrey.

'Seen much of this war?' asked Bone. He went through a series of prompts. 'Troop movements in the village. Black-out orders. Checking papers. So on and so forth. They took a couple of left-handed people away. Day before yesterday we had one of those Monet lily pictures delivered from New York, for safe keeping. Big as a hut! Thing is, so far, I haven't the least notion who the enemy is.'

'They'll find someone,' Susan assured him.

'Perhaps it's classified,' said Godfrey.

'Never thought of that!' said Bone.

I felt tired and I know from experience that in fatigue I am likely to fall. Sometimes exuberance vanishes like the puff of breath on a mirror, and horror comes back. 'I was hoping,' I said to Bone, 'we might have a session soon. One of the fifty-five-minute meetings,' I suggested.

'Oh, Lord, we won't fuss with those formalities, not now. You and I, we're always going to be talking – the way we do. No, I don't like the timed sessions or the thought that it's all going to be dealt with, tidied up. Most of the people I see they just want someone to talk to. Why not?'

'And the others?'

'Well, they have to be shut away. It's that or murder. Of course, people have the wrong idea of murder.'

'They do?'

'I think so. They're so used to regarding it as a crime – you know, the trial, the chair, the works. Load of talk for the newspapers. Murder is really just the idea of death.' There in a moment or so, casually, or so it seemed, Dr Bone had given me enough to think on for a year, or a lifetime.

'All of which reminds me,' he said. 'The Conference.' Vaguely, I remembered. 'Is Insanity in the Constitution – or is it Sanity?' He chuckled and winked at Susan who dropped a pretty little curtsey for him, like a shepherdess in a masque.

'Even at a time of incipient war?' I wondered.

'You have to press on with life,' said the resilient Bone. 'A hungry baby doesn't know there's an invasion scare. We've got people up in the west wing, wouldn't know what a war was if you showed them *Gone With the Wind*.'

I didn't know how to say it, he seemed so committed to the idea. But a conference did sound academic at a time when madness was about to be developed very earnestly.

'Are you giving a paper yourself?' I asked him.

'Thought I should: "Is the Pursuit of Happiness Certifiable?" You like that? I'll just wing it. Talk to them in a friendly way. That's all I ever do, really. You should come.'

'I should?'

'Certainly. Meet a few people. Burns is covering it for the radio, Johnson with the *Morning Post*, and that Orson Welles is set to speak – Halloween as a rite of fall, he's talking about. Supreme Court justices, too, a couple of them. It's going to be an event.'

'May I ask?'

'Shoot.'

'Will any of the speakers be inmates of the state?'

'You mean apart from the Justices? Hah! Got you there, didn't I?'

I had to tell him. 'You're an upbeat, Doc. I don't know why any of your patients would ever want to be cured.'

'Hush!' he said in an exaggerated espionage manner. 'Don't ever use that word with them. Upsets them terribly. They don't like to think about being cured.'

'That seems sad,' I said.

'The refusal to panic while handling unhappiness, that is a secret to life. Just find a storyline in chaos and stick to it.'

'That doesn't seem entirely American,' I said.

He began to laugh. 'First step in your new life, my boy,' said David Bone, 'realize you've never met *anyone* who is *entirely* American – apart from those ghosts on the screen.' More than ever, I felt myself in step with the Bone approach, no matter that in a ruse to defer his paperwork he cajoled me into one more twilight game of croquet. He demolished me, of course, chuckling all the way when he knocked me out of bounds and into the gloom, but I was happy with that.

So I thought.

* * *

Editor: *So happy you could fit this meeting in.*

Agent: *There is disquiet?*

Editor: *Well, marketing feels – just their lay opinion – that our author could actually be off his rocker.*

Agent: *His rocker or theirs?*

Editor: *Nice point. Theirs for sure – but I suppose they do rock our boat.*

Agent: But personally, you're steady with the author?

Editor: Oh, I am, but who am I?

Agent: You're troubled?

Editor: I don't know that I'd say troubled, but I am having difficulties.

Agent: Yes?

Editor: The fluctuations in period – the now and 1940. The calamity and the jokes side by side. The forest of movies. Plus we have found a startlingly low recognition number for poor Margaret Sullavan.

Agent: I believe that added to her dismay at the end.

Editor: Thing is, I like our author. We want to stand behind him. And we do see a nugget in the dark, shining like a torch. Rescue perhaps?

Agent: Oh, good.

Editor: That old idea of a book about kissing in movies.

Agent: Ah!

Editor: Scope for illustrations. Keep it to well-known pictures. And who doesn't enjoy a snog?

Agent: I see.

Editor: I wonder, could he be tactfully diverted into that? Keep his expertise but add a bit of sizzle?

Agent: Well...

Editor: Put it to him gently and let us do some scissors-and-pasting. There's this Madalena Vasco da Gama who would be prepared to do a bit of ghosting. She seems very talented.

Agent: I believe my client would be taken aback.

Editor: A rest perhaps?

Agent: Maybe.

Editor: The way he is, he might not even notice.

* * *

So it was, a few days later, that Dr Bone hired a motor bus in which we could be driven to a large and well-appointed country house just outside Waterbury. Doleful Norman was appointed as our driver, for he was good with vehicles and driving. Apart from him there were a dozen and a half of us, including the Bones, Godfrey and myself, Henry Spofford III and Fuck That, and several others I cannot recall now and who would only confuse you if the list was complete.

Our journey was interrupted from time to time by road blocks and halfhearted search procedures.

'Are those fellows Army?' Susan asked, 'Our Army?', and David answered, 'I think that's their uniform, but who knows?'

There were detours and a few freshly ruined buildings, though it was hard to tell whether shelling had done the damage or storms. We passed a column of refugees, but they lacked conviction, and might have been a hiking society out for the day had they not been struggling with large, scarred suitcases. They watched us in our bus but they did not wave or smile, and I thought I noted a surliness, an urge not to get out of the way of the bus.

'Looks as if it's happening,' said Susan. 'Resentment, and so on.'

Godfrey nodded. 'I've seen such things behind the lines on the Somme,' he said.

I was trying to steer the conversation round to hats when the crusty towers of buildings came in sight. The grounds were full of strolling conference members and the tennis courts had been made into a car park for the occasion. There were a few white tents on the lawn, marquees really, where different clinics and drug companies put on their show and offered refreshments. There was an amusing putting course and ponies ready to be ridden by the children.

'My dear,' said Spofford, 'have you ever been on a horse? Sidesaddle or Western?'

Fuck That shook her dour head, but answered, 'Have you ever eaten horse?'

'I wonder where Dr Dukenfield is,' said Bone. 'Chap in charge.'

No sooner mentioned than delivered, for an impresario in a white straw hat was strolling towards our bus. His walk wavered, I noticed, but nearly everything about this doctor strayed from the straight line. 'You are arrived!' he cried out, lifting his hat and letting us see the pomegranate glow of his face. He nearly tripped on a tuft of grass but steadied himself and was tip-top in his greeting to all of us. An aroma of the pickled grain arrived like a gathering of pollen in the air.

'Ah,' he said, '*les enfants*. How gratified I am to see them. And Mrs Bone – more radiant and rosy than ever, and thin, too.'

'You can't be too thin, Doctor,' she said.

'You can disappear,' said Dukenfield merrily (juggling was his hobby), though, in fact, Susan was nowhere near that fate. Dukenfield remained playful. 'Ah, madam, do not trifle with me. We all know that blush hue of yours masks the warmth of liquor.'

'Oh, Duke,' said Susan, 'don't be such a rotten tease.'

As if by gravitation, or some undetected affinity, Dukenfield drew near to Henry Spofford III, while looking askance at Fuck That.

'Well, little man, what is your name?'

'Henry, sir,' came the answer in a voice so close to gravel rattling in a bucket that Dukenfield stopped to examine the boy more closely. 'Melodious timbre,' he said. 'Do you practise it?'

'No sir, it is a natural thing.'

'Remarkable. As a rule I am averse to natural attributes. But yours is so odd.'

'It's an act,' said Fuck That.

Dukenfield turned to her with rather exaggerated surprise, as if he had not noticed her before. 'Truly? Well, what is your name, *petite fleure*?'

'I'm Susan, sir,' she said in a meek and ingratiating way. I was ashamed of her cunning.

Dukenfield sighed as if he was sniffing blossom. 'A sweet name,' he said. 'And you are Henry's pal and playmate?'

'Sir, I give him blowjobs from time to time. But he doesn't notice.' She would say anything – don't say I didn't warn you if she gets her own show.

'What an intelligent lad. I have always contrived to be otherwise occupied myself in those rapt moments. I study the *Racing News*.'

Is it dysfunction or the robustness of vagary and chance that apparently ill-suited people should fall so swiftly into alliance? Here they were, Dr Dukenfield and Fuck That, the kind of meeting over which onlookers winced in anticipation, yet a 'routine' arose that they both seemed to grasp. Had they played their scenes before? Was there some script in their inner workings? Just as my Connecticut companions appreciated so little after 1940 or so, I was helped to wonder – looking ahead – what obvious answers to life I was still unaware of. Did we all have relationships and scenarios stored in the billions of electrons in the brain? Were we written?

I once entertained the idea of doing a book about the weather. Wasn't it an international code? What put me off was the way it became a Big Subject with global warming and holes in the ozone, drought and rising sea levels, and so on. I didn't want the weather as done by Wagner or Bonaparte. I was more interested in a Noel Coward approach – the weather as small talk, and the sheepish way strangers could break a silence with 'Looks like rain?' or 'No, I fancy it'll clear up.' The interaction of weather and cricket or picnics was what intrigued me. Could one think of going out today, or was it a folly to do anything except prepare tea and crumpets, put more coal on the fire and watch the rain falling?

'Forecasts look splendid for the Conference,' said a cheerful David Bone.

'But isn't it held inside?' I wondered.

'Well, yes, that's correct. Can't have all the papers blowing away. Still, it's no fun sitting in the hall all day, is it? And then in the coffee break it's grand to get out on the lawns for a stroll and meet people. Discuss the topics, be collegial, gossip. Have I ever talked to you about light therapy?'

'Not once,' I said.

'Right you are. We have an agenda then for our next sit-down.'

'I would look forward to that.'

'You would? Might be up your street.'

'I prefer overcast light, if you know what I mean,' I said.

'That's the ticket!' cried Bone. 'By the way, do you have your ticket for the Conference sessions?'

'As a matter of fact, I don't,' I realized.

'You're spared then. Your lucky Conference.'

That was just a Bone pleasantry. No one was spared. Tickets spilled forth, like fake letters of transit. Before you knew it we were assembled, sitting in rows. Dr Dukenfield appeared, to introduce the proceedings wearing a tuxedo, as follows:

'When a grown man, your servant, puts on clothes like these to greet a company of friendly scholars, is it formality, politeness, a ploy to please the newsreel cameras – or is it one of those everyday displays of folly to which we are slaves?'

Whereupon he stripped to his gray long johns, and resumed. 'Or is this garb, which Dr Claude Dukenfield, yours truly, wears every day, comfortable, decent and appropriate – or has your servant been hitting the hard stuff?'

There was a rustle of applause, a good deal of laughter and a general turning to those sitting nearby to remark on the eccentric vivacity of Dr Dukenfield. Though a few were also of the opinion that he had been hitting the hooch. Indeed, there was a feeling that he had been hitting it so regularly that the hooch was now prepared to go quietly.

'Ladies and gents,' said Dukenfield, 'large questions and many others turn on this: Is our beloved United States so enthused with thoughts of democracy, justice, life, liberty and the pursuit of happiness that it embodies the best of man's reasoning? Or is the whole enterprise cockamamie?'

There was applause, though not everyone was up on that last word yet. His sour gaze was a clue to his own view. He bowed, and refreshed himself from a glass that was either cold tea, or not.

'In short, dear members of our Conference, is there room for insanity in our Constitution, or are we obliged as pilgrims in that illness to expunge it, to defy and deny it, and to keep any recidivists shut up for the rest of their natural? As it is, with war in the wind, we foresee the possibility of interning Germans, Italians, Japanese, Soviets, who knows where it will end? Should we therefore recommend more camps – hospitable, humane, with hot and cold running – so that even more of the disturbed and the unsound can be guarded? Will Connecticut be large enough? Or should we explore the possibilities in such begging expanses as Utah or Wyoming?'

I can't remember the whole thing, and you wouldn't want
me to. We had instructions what to do if an air-raid came,
and I had my hopes, but it never happened. Orson Welles did
arrive. Without notes, props, or a dame to saw in half, he stood
there in a burning white shirt and gave us his story about *The
War of the Worlds* back in '38 and how it demonstrated that
the American public was ready to believe anything; and if
that wasn't crazy, and hopeful, he didn't know what was.

A woman asked him whether he himself might not deserve
some of the responsibility for that devious adventure. 'Weren't
several people killed in the frenzy?' she wanted to know.

'Honey,' he said in a languid drawl, as a thundery look
brushed his baby face. 'I had no idea what would happen. I
thought it was just an honest Midwest trick-or-treat, done
on epic radio. Not one soul perished. Maybe a few innocent
people got in their cars and headed for the hills. That's an old
American custom, goes back to covered wagons and living
in the wilderness. Remember, this is a proud, ambitious and
savage society put down in the wilds bare moments ago. I have
come here to paint a picture for you of gullibility and those
lovely American ticket-buyers' – his voice dropped, the smile
fluttered, he was taking us into his generous confidence – 'the
suckers, ladies and gentlemen, thank you so much. I would be
nothing without you, my name is Orson Welles.' I saw how that
white shirt of his was dark now with sweat.

I happened to be near him as he made his way from the
podium to a waiting car, lifting up a young woman so lovely and
agile she could have been a ballerina. 'For God's sake,' I heard
him tell her, 'let's hang an exit and get back to Delmonico's.'

But there was a call for autographs, praise and stories about
how someone's aunt had been on the same trip to Germany
taken when Orson was a boy of twelve or so. And the chats
he'd had with Adolf, enough to inspire the shy German. Welles

agreed to everything but tried not to stop moving. The ballerina just gasped, as if in pain or ecstasy, and he lavished her with his fleshy smile. He dropped a kiss on her mouth and then repeated it so people could take their photograph. It seemed as if he might eat her.

'Don't run those pictures,' he implored. 'My wife won't understand.' And then a gale of laughter, the wind on which he finally got out of the place. The room was trembling as if a storm or a tremor had passed through it.

'My, my,' said Dukenfield, 'what a young magician he is – never gives a sucker an even break, don't you know. Did anyone say "lunch"?'

No one had uttered that word, but we trusted Dukenfield, and I went along with him to what I imagined would be an ample dining room. He turned to me, 'Did you enjoy the Kenosha kid?' he asked. I said I did. 'Of course,' said the doctor, 'I've had that turbulent ego in treatment for a year now. He only appeared today so I'd waive his bill.'

'Mr Welles is troubled?'

'Diddly-doo is what he is, my boy. Manic-depressive, they call it. German fellow thought of that, and now we're likely going to war with the Germans. What do you make of that? This Welles, he's up, he's down, he owes you half a crown.'

'But he's brilliant,' I said.

'Fellows like that, they use their mood as an elevator. Can't get out of bed. Can't stop talking about the future. He's a sick puppy and a great man. Can't have one without the other. Now, there, my friend, you have the real recipe of our disturbance. It's akin to the way I am an esteemed seer of society, while laboring under the reputation of a drunken ill-tempered sot.'

'That can't be so,' I protested.

'Have a care, sonny, I treasure the comfort in being unaccountable and unlikely. Do you by any chance have a flask of Laphroaig in an inside pocket? It is the only drink I trust apart from milk.'

I could not hide my surprise. 'You drink milk?'

Dukenfield staggered, as if a child, his own, had reviled and defamed him in a public square and then battered him with a large pillow. 'At long last, have you no decency, sir?'

TWELVE

The proceedings of the Conference are at last available, having gone from being banned and embargoed to becoming a sleeper bestseller with a rather garish cover. So it is not a wise use of our time, or of several white pages, to go over all that happened in detail. Such a survey will not make the event seem more likely, or less of a revelation of our many problems in the area of sanity and its variations. Much of the conference was soporific, and most of the rest of it was incoherent. Between Dr Dukenfield, young Orson and Justice Henry Julius there was a wasteland of annotated mediocrity and double-stitched innuendo. It is all there in the proceedings, even if they do more grinding to a halt than making progress.

In the matter of Justice Julius, however, we come upon a man of wayward genius mistakenly interpreted as disorder. In advance, it had been assumed by many that Justice Julius was from the US Supreme Court, the kahuna burger of courts. This was either a misunderstanding or a deliberate misrepresentation intended to boost attendance. Since Dr Dukenfield was central to the matter, I trust you to draw your own conclusions.

Justice Julius was in fact attached to the Connecticut Supreme Court which was at that time still known as the Supreme Court of Errors (that giveaway extra was deleted only in 1965, another era of turmoil).

On hearing that, you are going to throw this poor book down, in outrage, and say that the giddy limit has been exceeded. Look it up, sister! Pick the damn book up again! Nurse its wounded spine. The Supreme Court of Connecticut *was* once called the Supreme Court of Errors, which at least is more honest than some other supreme courts we have known.

Any disquiet there may have been in the assembly over Julius's credentials was quickly allayed by his striking appearance, somewhere between Shylock in an amateur production and something the cat had dragged in from the east end of the Bridgeport waterfront. He did look like a confidence man marinaded in doubt. Above all, one was alarmed by the size and assertiveness of his greasepaint mustache, lurking beneath such doleful, stricken eyes. The daub of 'tache was a wound or pubic roadkill. He was… well, what can I say when you have seen the pictures in the scandal magazines along with the accounts of his alleged misbehavior? These reports have had what I regard as a nasty edge to them, even if no charge leveled at Justice Henry so far is fully beyond the scope of human understanding (if you had a rotten upbringing – and many readers have).

Julius looked like a wolf shut out in the rain, like an exhausted orgiast, like… Oh, get on with it, man! So he decided to speak:

'Well, it's a nice surprise for me to be here, and you look startled, too. It's an honor, but I don't see much of that. Who does see much of Honor these days? And don't mention the nights.

'So, is Sanity in the Constitution, or is he in an institution? And if Santy is locked up we've got to get him free before Christmas or there are going to be mobs of children crying their eyes out. And kids in misery are a harbinger of a falling Dow and marked cards. Come to think of it why shouldn't the little rascals get used to unhappiness early? Why do we have wars, and famines and floods and football, if it isn't to teach them about disappointment? You see, once our founding fathers put happiness in the Constitution, seems to me they were guaranteeing the opposite. Isn't it a well-known law of metaphysics that if you ask for one thing you get the other? So the Constitution asks for liberty and ends up putting most of us in one institution or another, Sing-Sing or Cry-Cry, who can tell the difference? The Constitution sets out to give us reason, fairness and freedom, but it can't get cruel and unusual punishment out of its mind – especially for the poor. They deserve it, those wretches and spoilsports. What is "cruel" you ask – don't deny it madam, I could see you wondering. Well, we like to think that we all know what cruelty is, but let me tell you the onlooker believes it's one thing, while the victim knows something else. What does that tell you? There's the precious privacy of misunderstanding in our Constitution. You feel cruelty all on your ownsome. But the rest of the bums say it's a necessary punishment. Once upon a time there was hanging, drawing and quartering, and nowadays a quarter buys you nothing. Put a murderer in prison and it's more expensive than sending him to college. And in so many of our colleges he's mixing with riff-raff.'

Henry stepped back from himself for a moment, like a pole-vaulter in mid-air attempting fifteen feet for the first time (Cornelius Warmerdam had just cleared that height!), and realizing, yes, perhaps I can do it. All I have to do is learn to fly. And what is the role of pole-vaulting – except in prison escape movies – but to bring man closer to flight? He began again, but not before his artistic fingers reached up and gave his mustache a twirl. I swear I saw the first tender sprouting of growth amid the black greasepaint.

'So cruelty is the gateway to privacy and soon you find that backed up in the chance to follow a religion that's all your own, and only yours. It was privacy originally that no blacks, no women, no children, cats or dogs had the vote or a say. It was only for the club. Then there's the test of a "natural born citizen" being a requirement for the presidency. Some say that really means native born – born in the US– but it didn't say that. Said natural born, and I think it's clear what "natural born" excludes. At the time of the Revolution, most of the babies were born in their parents' home, or in a hole in the ground, the way wolves and bobcats were born. Natural meant no soothing drugs, no anesthesia, no Caesareans, no hospitals, no skilled staff, no mercy. Natural was taking your chances, and it wasn't thinking to plan or control the birth. So that outlaws any form of doo-dah, and means that the coming of an American president had to rely on copulation direct, *non interruptus*, and being delivered in a cold cabin on the prairie. It was a regime for mad men and women, too obedient to know any different way, short of murdering their guy.'

Was it his talk of wilderness, the atmosphere of growth, or could I actually see a real mustache growing on his upper lip like moss?

'This is the wilderness – and I include Connecticut as much as Nevada – where the vanity of men seeks to construct law and order. Well, you gotta have a few of those rules, like picking which side of the road to drive on and deciding that three of a kind beats two pairs. But rules are arbitrary, like tossing a coin. If two pairs beat three of a kind, I'd be in Tahiti in the lap of luxury, and the lap of Linda. The Bill of Rights and the Amendments may seem like rules for a game, but this American game is made up as we go along. Thus, good people (but I don't mind if you're rascals, sluts and whores – if you are, see me afterwards), originalism is a dam that will not stop the river of history. As far as we can, this nation protects aberration, waywardness, eccentricity and disorder. That pulse in our law and order is madness seeking to stand up for itself. Where do we feel it most? It is in that deluding encouragement to happiness, the thing that has made for more disturbance than whiskey, gin and sweet rum. That is the language of prohibition, but we are members of a land that would prohibit prohibition.'

Pandemonium in the hall, songs breaking out here and there, and an opportunity for Justice Julius to slake his thirst straight from a jug, wherein he expected to find not just water from the Connecticut River itself, but thick strands of bourbon, like red silk in the water. Refreshed, he resumed. But by now I was certain that a mustache as thick as lips and black as tar had replaced his masquerade. It shone in the damp of his drinking. It was a panther lurking in the darkness of his persona or his presentation. He was dangerous, and it seemed as if our rapt attention to his speech had brought that out in him.

'Finally, I would like to say a few words on the Second Amendment – words like humbug (are you kidding?) and persiflage. At this vexed moment, my fellow Americans, the nation faces another threat of war across the world. Giving offense to no one, we wait to be attacked. We are the sweet old lady in the park at dusk, but this old lady packs a punch like Dempsey! If we are drawn into that conflict, will we be content with a mere militia or shall we need an army? Won't we insist on a capital A Army? And as far as that body of fighting men is concerned, will we say to them bring your own guns, fellows – your personal weapons – or will we not behave like any responsible and deadly nation and distribute uniform rifles and medals, having made lucrative kickback contracts with the arms manufacturers? The militia, my friends, dates from the days of the earth closet, tooth extraction with a pair of pincers, and candlelight to read by. Originalism, if I may say so – and these are my closing words – is profoundly un-American in that it seeks to obstruct progress, changing your mind, the next pretty woman you see, and attractive openings with big business. So at the same time, the Constitution seems by necessity an original but inflexible document, but it is also an embodiment of second guessing, instability and constant departure from the dead order of Europe. This is America, ladies and gentlemen.'

The joy! The frenzy! The sale of refreshments! There was cheering in the room with hats, streamers, balloons and babies being tossed in the air and then slowly settling like sediment. If there was a war coming, God help the blithe upstarts who thought to oppose this exhilarated mob.

I was nearby when Dukenfield embraced Julius. 'Yes, sir!' roared the doctor. 'You stood up for folly! Folly and grandeur. You made me proud!'

Another development: what had been his shabby black suit, hanging from him like thrift-store rags on a refugee, stained and soiled, the black turning to verdigris, was now becoming a suit, a tailored, flattering uniform in which his body seemed full and fit and ready to fight. Designer fascism! As he was speaking, a nine and ten and then a twenty-seven and twenty-eight fell in behind him, their arms folded, guards and provocateurs, their leather like armor, so that their hands were clasped over their private parts, that essential fascist gesture. Justice Julius had become so impressive so quickly it had to be a matter of his confidence and our willing surrender. Cinna the Poet had turned into Caesar.

THIRTEEN

I was vibrating like timpani after that bizarre but electric speech by Justice Julius – and over-stimulation is not good for me. It's not that the event wasn't exciting and interesting, but for the first time I felt airlifted to the mood of 1940-41 and hearing an outrageous, intemperate speech that summoned belief in its listeners. It was as if I was perched on the brink of that old war, instead of any new catastrophe from my own time. But perhaps I was no longer sure what was my time. My being in Connecticut was no longer as a prisoner or a patient assigned there. I felt natural born to the state, even if it was the home of disturbance.

Did Godfrey guess at this? He sought to guide me away to empty places in the conference center, to be removed from the agitation of human company or its din. He wanted somewhere to sit quietly, not just to talk to me, but to be at rest and friendship.

We found a balcony that looked out on the gardens and the evening. It would be a perfect refuge for half an hour, before the dark, and so we sat down and subsided.

'I had hoped I had a treat for you,' said Godfrey.

'What's that?'

'An old friend. But perhaps he's been detained. You never know these days.'

Several minutes passed and I admit I was expectant. Then a man in a white dinner jacket came strolling through the gloom of the room behind us. I saw his jacket first, apparently moving on its own. He was lean, brisk and he had a trim mustache. He was preoccupied, too, as if he had an absurdly busy life barely kept under control. Still, he saw us and came over to chat. 'Anyone know when the dancing is going to begin?' he asked.

'Haven't heard about any dancing,' said Godfrey.

'I see,' said the man. He said his name was Biden, we should call him Eddie. Confidentially, he told us, he was putting a show together and hoping to turn up some talent. He was suave but natural, so we invited him to sit down. Then he clicked his fingers and another white coat came out of the shadows. This one was a waiter, so we ordered drinks. Whiskey for me, and a Manhattan for Godfrey, but Eddie said he'd take a beer and did they have a plate of sauerkraut? 'My wretched indigestion,' he explained. 'Thing about the war, if it comes, what scares me is this indigestion. How am I going to get the sauerkraut I need if it's in enemy hands?'

'Invade Germany?' suggested Godfrey.

'I say, I like that,' said Eddie. 'Fellow goes off to war for sauerkraut, or to retrieve a girl he used to know in Munich. Something that mocks the war and its pomposity. Might be nifty?'

'For a show?' I wondered.

'Or a picture,' said Eddie. 'Could be aces for Sully.'

We might have known. Biden knew Sully! Whereupon Godfrey admitted that the return of Sully was meant to be my surprise. 'I saw him earlier,' said Biden, 'with a girl. Diversions, you know.'

'Did you people hear that judge speak?' asked Eddie, sipping his beer and forking up the shining sauerkraut. 'Off his rocker. But there you are, he's a judge, so no one objects. Mad as a judge.'

'I don't know that one,' said Godfrey. 'Mad as a hatter, mad as a March hare, mad about the boy, mad as a wet cat, mad, bad and dangerous to know – never heard mad as a judge.'

'I'm interested in hats,' I said.

'Why not?' said Eddie, shifting in his chair to study me. It was as if a new item had arisen on our agenda. 'Talk about hats, please.'

'Well…' You know how it is, when you've been eager for so long to get into a subject, nursing it, and then, from out of the blue, the opportunity arrives, you're tongue-tied. But I rallied:

'I saw a tiny sculpture once – a manikin in a hat – and the hat came off, but it lifted the head with it. I thought that was telling.'

Godfrey chipped in as encouragement. 'I can remember parties at the Bullocks' on Park Avenue with a hundred hats lined up on a shelf, and I was expected to know which one belonged to which head. Of course, sometimes people went home with the wrong hat, but never mentioned it. If the hat fits, wear it. Don't we say that? If the head fits, wear it.'

'Laurel and Hardy,' said Biden and a fond chuckle circled the table like a round of bidding. It was all he had to say: certain truths hover in the air like fragrance.

I said, 'I have a suspicion that after the war – if this war does come – people will stop wearing hats.'

'How's that?' asked Godfrey. I didn't turn to him but I guessed he was giving me a watchful look. After all, a look is like a hat; it's something we try on to see if it works.

'Well, if millions have to wear heavy helmets in the war, when it's over they'll resent that habit. You look at Grand Central at rush hour, now, it's a sea of hats bobbing along. After the war, I suspect, we won't trust a hat to protect us. We'll want people to look at our heads, our faces, to look at us.'

I'd gone too far, I realized, yet Godfrey was the only one who seemed to notice it. And if I had had the feeling for days of being trapped in this past of theirs, it wasn't so surprising that someone as alert as Godfrey might feel I had an odd aura of a future about me.

'This war,' he said, quietly, 'how do you see it turning out?'

'How would I know?' I said. I wanted to drop the subject.

'If we lose our hats, will we lose anything else?' Godfrey wanted to know.

'Possibly,' I admitted. 'Innocence might slip.'

'Can you call us "innocent" now?' asked Eddie. 'I'd say we're pretty damned cynical.'

'We're children, still,' I wanted to explain. 'Every age reckons it's cynical or sophisticated, then thirty years later they look like infants.'

'Will this war be nasty?' Godfrey persevered.

It was quite dark by then. We could not really see the expressions on our own faces. 'Why not?' I admitted. 'Worse than we know? Unexpected revelations.' *You* know how much more I could have said. But there was no point in offering warnings, and I didn't want to be depressing, or spoil the ending.

At that moment the sound of music began in another room. It felt like a large band – saxes and brass, hand in glove, like Glenn Miller – and lights sprang up in the great room behind us. Despite the anticipation of a devastating war, the music was nostalgia for the best years of our lives.

'Aha, the dancing,' said Eddie, a look of anticipation in his eyes. He had been waiting for it. 'A String of Pearls,' 8 November 1941. The last poised moment?

'Sad thing about Glenn,' I said, too moved to stay discreet.

'How so?' asked Godfrey. He was intent on me now, but still I didn't face him.

'That plane crash,' I said. Perhaps I looked like a dreamer.

'Glenn Miller? You've got the wrong person, I think. Don't you mean Carole Lombard?'

'Ah yes, of course,' I corrected myself. He smiled, and it was only later that I realized why he might have seemed sad and fond. But he did look at me as if he was beginning to see our end game.

Eddie was getting up and starting to dance with an imagined partner, holding on to emptiness. 'I love Carole Lombard,' he said. 'Who doesn't adore her?'

As we came closer to the ballroom, the music changed and we heard a female singer start up with, 'I'm Through with Love…' It was an immature voice, yet touched by the dismay of the song.

The voice belonged to a blonde sitting on a piano in front of the band, propped up on her hands. Already there were people dancing, conference participants letting down their hair, but some of them were looking at this lush singer more than at their partners. The woman had the widest eyes. I felt I could drive an automobile through them. But the eyes were a battleground for hope and experience, and hope was accustomed to losing. 'I could put *that one* in a movie,' said Eddie, talking to himself.

My thoughts of war and shifting times vanished. This was the kind of woman you see in cartoon strips, or hear about in dirty jokes from comedians. She was the sort that soldiers pin up on their walls for the duration or carry in their wallets from the Halls of Montezuma to wherever it is. But here she was, her hair like platinum in the spotlight and the custard of her soul on the point of pouring out of her sketchy dress. She said she was 'through with love', but most men would have vowed, 'Not yet'.

I saw Henry Spofford III dancing with Fuck That. He was upright and rigorous in his foxtrot and she let everyone see how delighted she was by her earnest stooge. She seemed devoted to him now, and once or twice I read her lips saying, 'Yes, dear', after some of his lugubrious statements. I had an odd sensation that they were my own parents when young – her flighty, him stalwart and single-paced.

There was an announcement that the dance would go on as arranged, even though an outbreak of hostilities was said to be imminent. Dr Dukenfield himself, I heard, had left the premises in his Duesenberg. Then came a report that he had crashed into a tree less than a mile away and been taken into custody for driving under the influence. But Justice Julius put in an appearance, with a tall, stout and very dignified woman on his arm. Asked whether this was his wife, he promptly slapped the questioner in the face with a folded dance-card. 'This is my mother,' he said, 'Madam, do you have to dog my steps? Why not take that dog for a walk? You see how I am being made ridiculous in this process?'

'In that matter, you are a self-made man,' said his imperious companion, or whatever she was.

And still that blonde was singing to the room. I daresay some in the throng were oblivious, but Godfrey and I were paying her close attention. There was something so mythic about her, so complete, that I think we both feared she might crack, like the shell of an egg. But then she moved, or turned against the clingy fabric of her dress and it was evident that she was more than the shell. She was the egg.

'A rare creature,' said Henry Spofford III. He must have noticed our role as her audience, for he walked up to us to share in our gaze.

'You appreciate her already?' asked Godfrey.

'Owing to an encounter I have already had with her,' explained Spofford.

'You know her?' I cried.

'True knowing would require many years,' said Spofford, 'and she may not last that long.'

'But you met her. You've spoken to her?'

'In the hotel yesterday,' he began. 'I came upon her attempting to leave a room by a small side window. I cannot estimate why. Her treasured fanny was caught in this porthole, but by a series of maneuvers I contrived to cover for her and facilitate her escape. She said she would be forever grateful to me, and she dropped a kiss on my cheek.' He took a white handkerchief from his pocket and showed us the winged imprint of a day-old pink kiss. 'I thought it wise to remove the evidence, before my Susan noticed.'

'She'd have your guts for garters,' surmised Godfrey. He was looking at the singer while he spoke to Spofford.

'Ah,' said the child. 'She has had them before.'

He appreciated our admiration, even if it was an urge that had not fully possessed him yet. 'You want to meet her?' he asked.

So this stilted boy with the groaning voice led us towards the band and waved his hand at the singer. She seemed to be on a break and she swayed towards us because of high heels beneath the figure eights of her body. What was more remarkable was that, as she came closer – and Godfrey told me later that he had felt the same thing – there was an increase of warmth in the air. Was it physical? I'm sure it was, but it was emotional, too.

'Oh, hi,' she said, as Spofford introduced us. 'If you're friends of Mr Spofford, I'm on your team. I hope you'll forgive me for perspiring. I get warm when I sing. It can be embarrassing.'

'Not a problem in the world,' said Godfrey.

'One time in New York in May – it was a birthday party – I could hardly bear to keep my clothes on.'

I plunged in – always saying these reckless things. 'Well, if you can't bear it, you have to bare it.'

'What?' She looked at me as if I had dropped into a foreign language. Then like an old, slowmo computer, her synapses seemed to bump together. There was sluggish dawn in her eyes. 'Was that a pun? I never know.'

'Puns lie thick on the ground like autumn leaves.' Who do you think said that? There's no prize, but it was Henry Spofford III as if auditioning for the role of the wise man in *Lost Horizon*.

'Don't you love the way this kid talks?' said the blonde. 'That's a voice loaded with rueful experience.' She shivered: 'Oh, it turns me on.'

'Stop that whispering, child,' said Spofford. 'If you find me attractive, just admit it.'

'You see!' she was delighted. 'Voices are it for me. I like the voice when I can't understand what it's saying. I have slept with some voices, you know.'

'Sounds like *Gentlemen Prefer Blondes*,' observed Godfrey.

She was wide-eyed: 'Guys will go for any color, anything that's awake, and not always that, let me tell you. Musicians are the worst. I have these two guys in the band, hounding after me – tenor sax and bass fiddle. The trickiest thing about singing is the musicians. But, believe me, trumpet-players can kiss!'

'When you sing, you get hot?' said Godfrey, like a discerning doctor.

'Right! Did I tell you that? It's true. My body is my worst enemy. I have tried to get rid of it two times.'

'How do you do that?' I asked.

'When she goes to bed,' said Spofford, 'she hangs her clothes up in the closet, and then she puts her body in a plastic clothes bag. The ones with the zipper.'

'Oh Spoff, you are so cute, I adore you. Hurry up and get legal, honey. I don't know how long I have. He is such a gentleman,' she said to us.

Indicating Godfrey, I told her – I had to – 'Do you realize, he was a gentleman's gentleman.'

'Oh wow! That is very impressive.' It was not that she was showing a trace of disloyalty to Henry Spofford III, or that she ceased generating waves of carnal benevolence as far as anyone was concerned, but I think she saw the possibility, indeed the logic, of being with Godfrey. And so you may have gathered by now, the thing with Connecticuts is their yearning for love, marriage and remarriage. They do divorce because it lets them woo their ex again. I have been that fickle myself, but I thought by then that if I had been brought to Connecticut in a free limo, wasn't it about time I got a little treatment?

'You're the author,' said Godfrey – not in a reproachful way – 'if you need it, have yourself some treatment. What sort of doctor would you want?' He had the air of being an agent for anything I might need.

'Well…'

'Man or a woman?'

'Let me –'

'Young or old?'

'Not a novice, but someone with experience who can stay awake.'

'Austrian or American? Freudian or Hollywood? Texas hold 'em or five-card draw?' So many questions to be decided.

Suddenly I remembered. 'Isn't there a Dr Spielrein? Didn't she practice with Jung? Russian, perhaps, but trained in Switzerland? I've heard good things about her.'

'I believe that's right,' said Godfrey. 'Unusual woman. Not approved by everyone, but I hear that practice worked out in the end. Novel therapy, with exercise.'

'Physician, heal thyself,' said the blonde, and she told us to call her Sugar.

'Look, I have to do another set,' she said. 'Can we get together later? And I do mean you,' she said, pointing her finger so that it prodded Godfrey's stiff white dickey. He chuckled bashfully and before we knew it she was into 'My Heart Belongs to Daddy', with just one wink over the blancmange crest of her shoulder.

FOURTEEN

Later than most people, I noticed how life in Connecticut was winding down. About time, too, for the outer world was hurrying towards its own crisis. There were aircraft in the sky every day now as well as the procession of refugees who had little idea where they were supposed to be going. You could imagine an ending coming, even if you had no clue what to feel about it.

Godfrey and Sugar seemed content in the arrangement of a gentleman's gentleman and his lady. He was courtly with her; he gave her time; he saw the best in her; and he encouraged her to discard her little girl voice and to speak in her own artless Californian way (more Thermal than Bel Air). She was taken aback to be treated in this manner, and there were signs that she was opting now for domesticity. She made cakes and pies, like Mildred Pierce, that role model of 1941.

For a short time, those two musicians she had warned us about tried to sneak her away. They were scoundrels, and conspirators. Sugar forgot their names, but she said it didn't matter because they were giving up show business ('before it dumps them, you ask me') and talking to each other as thirty-one and thirty-two. So their tuxedos turned into the black suits of menace.

Could Godfrey look after Sugar? I couldn't tell, but I suppose when you see your child married off there is the same unease and a matter of crediting the child's happiness while searching their eyes for a hint of waiting to be rescued. Godfrey was too old for war service, or too sophisticated. The bravado of combat would have deflated under his irony. But where would they go if Connecticut became a war zone? How would they know which side of the lines to be? I was fond of them both. Godfrey was experienced and he had the wisdom of a survivor. But Sugar… well, she was either an empress or a victim. One look at her and you wondered how long she could last.

Irene was dead; Cornelia was caught up with Vincent, or with a line of Vinces, nurses she could suck into that clinic. David and Susan Bone had their own establishment, or perhaps it had been destroyed by now. Would they notice? I don't mean that facetiously but it was Bone's strength to ignore the bad things and keep a cheerful eye on prospects.

I did speak to Henry Spofford III. I asked him if he thought he and Fuck That should stay with me, to be cared for. If that's what they wanted to call it, or if they thought I offered care.

'Well, where are you going, sir?' asked Henry.

'I'm not sure. I have to be treated, I suspect. I can't see why I was brought here if not for that.'

The boy studied me. He was learning. Had this old child been waiting for me? He considered the matter, and maybe matters I could not imagine. 'Then we might only be encumbrances to you.'

I protested that, but he was too much of a wise grandfather figure to be denied.

'I pray you, sir,' he said. 'Nothing will encourage us more than knowing you are taking the best care of yourself. Of course, we will provide for Baby.'

The leopard looked up at us; this seemed to be the best day in its odd life.

Even Fuck That had a brief, 'Miss you, nuncle,' and a damp, cold kiss on my lowered cheek. I would have told her to write but I remembered that she couldn't.

Eddie Biden had gone away and Sully was still nowhere to be seen. I played with the idea that those two might meet up – in Providence or Palm Beach – and be useful for one another. A place where Eddie could get beer and sauerkraut – I think he was a pale ale man, with mustard in the mayo on the cabbage. We recall the small details.

So I turned to my own condition and wondered how I might find that Dr Spielrein – Sabina Spielrein – and her unusual reputation. The last I had heard this doctor was in Russia and the idea of phoning that country and asking for her had a cockeyed charm but not much practical possibility. Then my phone rang. It was a friendly, but cool voice, with a Russian accent, but perfectly clear.

'This is Dr Spielrein.' (Look, this is a book.)

I was amazed and one can do or say foolish and involuntary things then, like sneezing or seeing the light.

'A Mr Godfrey suggested I call you. He said you might be too nervous to phone yourself. That is right?'

'He's correct in most things,' I said.

'Aha. He said he was a close friend. So we should meet, don't you think?'

'I thought you would be in Russia.'

'Sabbatical. I am here to write a report. The Soviet Union, you see, has been developing Siberia as our Connecticut. We are eager to share data.'

We met next day at eleven in her large office at Yale. She was... no, I must begin again. She was... this is more difficult than I anticipated.

Look, I fell in love with her in about 11 seconds. (If it takes too long, I am not inclined to trust the interaction.)

She was petite, slender, walnut dark in her hair and eyes, but with a junket-white skin. Did I say beautiful? Yet I'm not sure that that was what I noticed first – it could have been

her dominating at-first-sight eyes with their piquant hint of
ruin. (Another Margaret Sullavan part!) In addition, she was
wearing a costume of 1912 or so – a full-length pleated skirt
in white linen and a cream-colored cotton blouse buttoned up
to the throat. Then there was her jaw. It jutted forward like the
bowsprit of a clipper ship, or like a spade about to dig your
grave. The effect was daunting yet alluring.

'Very well,' she said. 'We should proceed quickly, I think.'

'You have to go back to Russia?' I was apprehensive.

'I am thinking this war may arrive at any moment. There are
so many rumors. Aren't you watching for it, night and day?' I
felt she had her own worries: of course, doctors do.

She noted my relevant personal information, though she did
not seem impressed. 'You do understand,' said Dr Spielrein,
'that at some point in our consultation, I shall require you
to rebuke me. This is not in the textbooks, but it is normal
procedure for me. Just my way, no need to be alarmed. It
sharpens my insights. Is that clear?'

'Here? In this room?'

'Of course. We will not be disturbed. I will remove my
clothing for that purpose, and I will not resist, though I may
cry out. It is not personal. But you must not take pity on me, or
be weak about it. And then – leave this possibility open, we play
it by ear – but you may care to be conjugal with me. Sometimes
this happens. Forcefully if you like, though tender is OK, too.'

I'm sure I revealed my dismay as much as my excitement.
'But the patient-doctor relationship,' I said. 'Isn't such a thing
forbidden? Isn't it taboo?'

She smiled to herself. 'Taboos are to be tested. They would
not be taboos without intense attraction. Say the word, "taboo"
– is it not haunting? If you run away from them, they will turn
up everywhere. Isn't that comical? Oscar Wilde said he could
resist everything except temptation. Did you know him?'

'I don't know. I feel at a loss.' Would I have to administer a whip? Personally? Instead of just watching?

'Well,' she said, she seemed disappointed, 'take it or leave it. I don't think it's so much to ask. I will not be charging you. I doubt I can even put in for expenses. And whatever you feel about it, I do need to be punished. You can say that's improper, but I function so much better if that occurs. It clears my mind and reminds me of duty. I only want to do the best for you. Shall we get it over with?'

Not that we rushed. She stepped out of her day clothes and was wearing just a white corset, a milky bustier and a white cotton petticoat. She then stretched out her body along the length of a couch and left me to apply the short, flayed whip. Of course, I went too easily at first and she had to say, 'No, no, soft heart. More firmness, please.' Soon I was finding my touch and I could hear her gasp after the snap of the whip. There were raspberry lines on her back and the whip broke off one hook-and-eye fastening on her bustier. She had the look on her face of someone who might have just run a marathon, and won it.

A little out of breath, she said, '… ten, eleven. That was excellent. You picked it up quickly. Thank you so much for your kindness. Would you wish to take me completely now?'

I said I would be embarrassed, I would rather talk, so she put on her clothes, rebrushed her hair, and asked me to sit on the couch where she had been thrashed. 'Now then,' she said, picking up a pencil and a notepad. 'I feel refreshed. Do you understand why you were sent to Connecticut?'

'No one has ever told me,' I said.

'The method here is for patients to brood on a question, and discover an answer within themselves. Do you understand?'

So I began, like someone in a novel after the novelist has made the specious claim, 'Well, really, my characters acquire a life of their own. And I only channel it.'

'Of course,' I lied. I said... I added that... Which reminded me of... But as I warmed to the role, I saw new possibilities. 'You know,' I said to her demanding stare into my timid face, 'I do wonder if I'm making this up for you, because I like you.'

She was like a mongoose with a snake. Her smile was so understanding. 'You can't lie, dear sir. That is what is so clever about stories. When people talk about themselves, they are guarded and invariably they lie, but the lies reveal as much as the truth. When you tell a story, you see, you open up and defenses disappear. If you say you are the Tsar's lost son, that is fanciful but significant – because some idea of the Tsar or loss stirs you. So few people say they want to be their father's son! Many Russians once dreamed of being Tsar, and now that dream is forbidden.'

'I wanted to be great but I realize I am abject?' I suggested.

'Or you try to be nothing, but you cannot stop your own regal nature from surfacing.'

I was being offered a fuller possibility of myself than ever before. That is the test, and most of us dodge it – but then complain about it never coming along.

'You say you are writing a book about the kiss in movies?'

'That's right.'

'Intriguing subject. The kiss can be so mysterious. It is a big thing, isn't it? Mouth to mouth. And needing to be risky. Will movies last, do you think? Not as long as the mouth? Do you have your book with you? I would so like to see it.'

'I had to leave it when they came to bring me to Connecticut. It couldn't be helped.' I felt such a failure for her.

'So, it's... at home?'

'It must be.'

'Aha,' she was writing this down carefully. 'Yet I think you do not have a home.' She was being tender, I knew, whether to respect homelessness or my misrepresentation. 'The paperwork says that you were collected by car from a library. Like a book? It says nothing about home. Of course, these days paperwork is not always to be trusted.'

'Ah,' I said. I might have been stabbed. She seemed to be giving me questions, but really they were answers. Who would not fall in love with that?

'So, you would like to be in a movie kissing someone?' suggested Dr Spielrein. She was enchanting when she was being professional.

'Or kissed, perhaps,' I said.

'Ah yes, kissed by someone else? Some Margaret Sullavan?'

'I don't know if I have the energy to do it myself.'

'And you have no name?'

'No need,' I said.

'Really? We could give you a name. Like parents with a child.'

'Do you have children?' I asked her. I could feel a maternal edge in her.

'Two. Renata and Eva. They are in the Soviet Union. How do you feel now?'

'The same as always,' I said. 'Often I hardly exist. I don't want to be with people, real people. I would like to be invisible. I feel alone. But then sometimes I think I could own the world and all its adventures. I have an exhilarating sense of *anything* being possible. I say impulsive wild things, inappropriate things. Things that do damage. I am a hero and a murderer at the same time. And then I slip back to being nothing.'

She was looking at me in wonder and affection. 'Do you realize how engaged you become in talking about this? It is the strong part of bipolar,' she said. 'We are getting along so very well. Sometimes all this takes years.'

'Is there any cure?' I asked.

'Oh no, there is never a cure. It is a normal condition. Like being tall. You realize, I like to be beaten. People tell me this is bad, unhealthy and so on. I would not want my daughters to know about it. My husband has declined to assist me. So I must find polite strangers who will do it. I think I need the shame. I became an analyst. Meeting strangers and being a useful stranger to them. I have tried not to, but I cannot stop. Perhaps you would thrash me again now. Please?'

So I did it. We had a system already: the removal of her day clothes; the tidy folding of them; the snowy surprise of her undergarments; the whip in my hand; her stretched out body – like someone on the rack; her jaw thrusting out and up like a child learning to swim; her gasps and the sound of the whip; the lines on her back criss-crossing. My own regret and its opposite. The shy feeling of necessary power. And once, her head turned aside to look up at me, smiling with delight, her eyes aglow – as if the child had learned to swim. Her feet were off the bottom.

We did then enter into a fumbled sexual act. (I knew her better by then – she had my secrets without giving way to scorn or pity.) It was nothing to write home about, and there was no home anyway. It was kind, clumsy and amusing. We laughed a good deal, but were we laughing at the same things? Who could tell? Were we making love? I mean, did our efforts have an end-product, a recognizable commodity, like picked cotton or chopped wood? Or was it merely a means of being able to talk?

'That was nice,' she said. There was a smell of Viennese pastries on her skin. Almond, I guessed.

'It was? I am by no means an expert.'

'So long as no one insists on being an expert,' she said, 'it can be quite pleasant.'

I slept, and when I woke, she was humming a song, or working at it.

'What's that you're humming?' I asked.

'I was copying you,' she explained. 'You were singing in your sleep.'

'It sounds like "Rescue Me" by Fontella Bass.'

'I have not heard of her.'

'Oh,' I murmured drowsily with a confidence I could not muffle, 'she'll be big one day.'

'One day? What one day is that, my friend?'

Look, I was drunk on romance, which I was not used to. It was like giving a kid champagne. I meant no harm. I suppose I just hoped to impress this Dr Spielrein. 'In '65,' I guessed.

Talk about your spontaneous, reckless remarks! There was silence for a while, and I hoped she had not noticed. But when I looked at her grave eyes, that chance was gone. She was gazing at me with poised wariness, as if she had entered her own house and come upon a leopard on the sofa.

'You see the future?' she asked. She didn't know whether to laugh or cry, and there was trepidation in her voice. 'Mr Godfrey told me there might be something unusual about you.'

'I guess at things, that's all.'

She was deciding whether to ask me something. I knew how her mind worked now – what an analyst! One who can aspire to wholeness while being driven on by damage. Should I remind you that one of Dr Spielrein's most important papers was entitled, 'Destruction as the Cause of Coming Into Being'? It would be seen as one of the first descriptions of a death instinct directing life's energy.

At last she spoke. 'Well then, my dear, guess what may become of me, please.' Such a face – such a question, a Russian Jew wondering about 1942: these are things that represent the war to anyone looking back. But she was looking forward.

'You?' I had to seem to be pretending or guessing in the dark. 'Do you intend to go back to Russia?' I felt the helpless sadness of that destiny, the feeling of all those lives in the night.

'I must. I have my patients, and my children are there. The war will come to Russia.'

What would you have done? I made a game of it, or I tried. I said, well, be careful of 1942 – like watch out for the big bad wolf.

'That's soon,' she said and I heard brave fear in her voice. August 1942, I thought, but I didn't dare admit that to her – anyway, my history of the Holocaust was not tidily filed.

'What happens?' she asked. She was trying to keep knowledge under a tight rein. 'How would I know?,' I said helplessly. But I supposed to myself that there could be units of German forces – let's call them Einsatzgruppen A or B, or C or D.

'Is there a place called Zmievskaya Balka, perhaps,' I said. 'I made that up,' I added quickly, and I tried to smile. I had invented a deliberate muddle from a foreign language.

'You may have concocted that name,' said Sabina, 'still, it means ravine of snakes. It is near Rostov-on-Don. I know it already. We have a house nearby, a little place in the country.' She was calm and still. We were side by side in her narrow bed in all the white of fresh sheets. She loved laundry. I could smell our bodies: strudel and the sea.

I felt dizzy; I could not tell whether it was dread on her behalf or giddiness at crossing the timeline. 'Oh, don't go there,' I begged. I whispered like a child in childish make-believe. Are lost loves as piercing as those found? Or do they last the longest?

'I have to,' she answered, and her face now was so thoughtful it seemed older. Then she smiled. 'But when I do, I will think of you.'

That smile did nothing to heal her or alter her destiny. She was a scientist, to be sure, with years of study and degrees. Her work is as remarkable as her life. A lover to Jung, a friend to Freud, and finally the victim of Adolf – as well as solace to your author. She had trained herself to be rational, but she had an imp of humor in her. She did not disown that urge to be thrashed and then to plunge into embracing her punisher. So she knew how much leeway an analyst had to allow for darkness or privacy. And while she was an alert gambler with her future, she seemed to recognize some likelihood in the story I had sketched. She did not lie to herself.

I never mentioned her children or the 27,000 killed by the Germans (I looked this up later – it is there), the men shot, the women gassed. As if counting could contain it. I said nothing, but stroked the staring cheeks in which her eyes waited.

The next day, I was thinking so much about Sabina Spielrein, I did not notice Sully on the street corner.

'Hey, buddy, you going to pass me by?' he called out. He was sitting on a fire hydrant, counting his toes.

'Not at all,' I assured him. He had his bum's clothes still, though they were the worse for wear now. He had his trusty ash stick and his bundle of possessions.

'I don't much reckon the idea of hanging around here,' he said. 'This Connecticut thing, peace and healing, I think that number's up.'

'Really?'

'Last few days I've seen bad stuff in this war of theirs. Troop movements, refugees. Corpses piled like firewood. The old dread. Saw a firing squad, kids worn out from shooting. Couple of villages disappeared.'

'How do we pick a safe way to go?' I wondered. A horse was wandering loose in the street, with an open wound in its haunch. No one did anything.

Sully was studying the animal, too. 'Well, look at it this way, pal, lots of the maps have been withdrawn. If anyone wins this war they'll forbid 'em altogether. We may forget the shapes and the look of country we loved. Evenings in the woods. But is that a reason for not setting out? Time comes, you need to make your move, walk across a meadow, into the trees. That a whip you've got in your hand?'

'Something I picked up,' I said, and I dropped it there on the street. I saw a red smear on the lash, and hesitated. But Sully and I started walking; we went together, and thought to quit the state of Connecticut and its memories. Of course, I am lying to you about the memories. I always remember Sabina Spielrein's future.

Am I better than I was when kidnapped for Connecticut? I don't know, and I don't know who would know. But I do not expect to get out of Connecticut or its possibility. Despite its apparent boundaries, the state and its condition stretch far and wide and contain so many of us.

'No ashes, no coal can burn with such glow as a secretive love of which no one must know.'

Sabina Spielrein, diary, 22 February 1912

''Cause I'm lonely
And I'm blue, I need you
And your love too
Come on and rescue me.'

– Fontella Bass

CLUES, or SUSPECTS

Sully is Joel McCrea in *Sullivan's Travels*

Alice Swallow is Virginia Walker, David Bone is Cary Grant, Dr Fritz Lehman is Fritz Feld, and Susan is Katharine Hepburn, in *Bringing Up Baby*

Horace Pike is Eugene Pallette, Lady Eve Sidwich is Barbara Stanwyck, in *The Lady Eve*

Irene Bullock is Carole Lombard, Alexander Bullock is Eugene Pallette, Angelica Bullock is Alice Brady, Carlo is Mischa Auer, Godfrey is William Powell, Cornelia Bullock is Gail Patrick, in *My Man Godfrey*

Ned Merrill is Burt Lancaster, in *The Swimmer*

Grady is Philip Stone, in *The Shining*

Lilith is Jean Seberg, Vincent is Warren Beatty, Dr Brice is Kim Hunter, in *Lilith*

Henry Spofford III is George Winslow, in *Gentlemen Prefer Blondes*

Norman is Anthony Perkins, in *Psycho*

Dr Claude Dukenfield is WC Fields

Orson Welles is as ever Orson Welles

Justice Julius Henry is Groucho Marx in his collected works

Edmund Biden is Preston Sturges

Sugar Kowalczyk is Marilyn Monroe, in *Some Like It Hot*

Dr Sabina Spielrein is Keira Knightley, in *A Dangerous Method*

TALKING TO THE AUTHOR

I wondered as I was reading, why you chose Connecticut as the lucky or unlucky state.

Several screwball films are set there. I think the state was an inviting hideaway place for New Yorkers. So many creative people in the city – in the arts or their business – liked to get away for long weekends. They could feel they were in the country. But still close to New York. It was a kind of paradise, reliant on the railway and the phone. All those things were in play, but I must admit to another guiding force. I was fascinated by the word, and its two parts – 'Connect' and 'I cut'. Maybe this is crazy but I felt a tug of war in that: being together and being apart.

Craziness is not inappropriate in this case. Let me ask you about another word – 'Screwball' – what does that mean for you?

It's the term we use for a genre in which comedy begins to crack open because the characters are really disturbed – if that's the word. It's not just the fools in screwball. The world has gone daft.

Our words for this mood are so uneasy – insane, crazy, demented, all feel very final, but they could be foolish, 'not quite himself', or disturbed. Words we can get along with.

And I think that having money (or not) was vital in how story treated the disturbed. If you were rich enough you could be 'eccentric'. If you lacked resources, the same behavior might get you confined – in your own home, or in an institution. But we are smart enough now, or uneasy enough, to wonder if the allegedly disturbed people may not be the ones who have seen how deranged the society is. You can say the madhouse is where we all live.

So madness can be visionary or poetic? And your book slips from being madcap and funny to madhouse and very frightening in a way that is not just the early 1940s. It could be now.

Which reminds me. I had a terrible sense of Connecticut being the right place when I heard about the school killing at Sandy Hook. That was coincidence, I suppose, and we have had so many mass killings, but literally that news came in as I was preparing to write. The prospect of a school where the children would be armed in self-defense – that is surely madness. Though some people propose it.

But just in your way of separating Connect and I cut, screw and ball are suggestive.

Yes, two sexual verbs, and throughout the screwball genre there is this feeling of sexual desire struggling to get free. All these films were done under censorship, of course, but I think that was very helpful. The desire is the greater for being smothered. In *Bringing Up Baby*, David and Susan are totally unsuited, but they can't ignore their attraction. In that first meeting at the country club, he accidentally removes some of her clothing. If you believe in accidents.

And smacks his hat against her exposed ass to rescue her.

So protective, so erotic. One of the sexiest moments in American film. Like the scene in *The Lady Eve* where the card-sharp seduces the stuffed shirt, Stanwyck and Henry Fonda.

And the 'I' character in your book, the fellow who is dragged away from writing a book about the kiss in movies, he is consumed with desire. How far is that you?

Let's say it's a mocking version of me, and that breed of us that has spent half our lives in the dark fantasizing over the light. Even now, one point of *Connecticut* is a film historian urging readers to go see these movies that are very old, in black and white and rather silly. But I think my own process of desire was led on by movies, and I'm not sure I feel at ease over that. Desire can be dangerous.

But maybe these are the best movies Hollywood ever did?

I think so. The other genres seem stale now, but screwball is endlessly mysterious and suggestive just because these wild urges of desire are burrowing away. A lot of the crazy things sane people do come from a desire that won't behave.

There are two women in the book who are remarkable objects of desire. Margaret Sullavan. She gets an interlude to herself.

I always wanted to write about her – wooing her, I daresay – ever since I saw *The Shop Around the Corner* and read *Haywire*, the wonderful book by her daughter Brooke Hayward.

A few of us are still crazy about her.

For sure, but you understand that falling in love with people on a screen, people who are likely dead – it is sort of certifiable.

But you use the figure of Jed Harris to show us how desire destabilized her.

That's it. Beauty and the beast.

Would you have slept with Sullavan?

In terror.

Did you say 'error'?

I thought I said 'terror', but maybe I was mistaken.

And Dr Sabina Spielrein – I had never heard of her.

Neither had I, until I saw *A Dangerous Method* where she is played by Keira Knightley. If you recall, she is a patient who has a passionate affair involving violence with Jung (played by Michael Fassbender). She was a real person, even if she was Jung's fantasy. She went on to an illustrious career in psychiatry. She was a fine writer and very discerning. And, yes, she and her children were murdered by the Nazis in the way described in this book.

You make it clear that you have manipulated her as a character. She appears magically and you tell us, 'Look, this is a book.' But I think she is very touching.

The more I discovered about her the better I liked her. And there's something rare in the way Knightley plays her. An awkward intensity.

There's a note of possible rescue throughout the book. It's there in the Fontella Bass song, 'Rescue Me'. Do you think the movies rescue us? Can that happen?

We don't seem to be rescued, do we?

So you've done these three books over a period of time – Suspects, Silver Light *and* Connecticut, *film noir, the Western and screwball – and in all of them a movie genre is like a country we have entered and lived in. Is that your America?*

I don't think we can tell yet, and maybe we never will. But I do feel the culture of movies amounted to the chance that desire could be fulfilled. And that was a religion, or a climate of faith. We call it the American dream, but the dream needs to be interpreted.

And the books are etched in doubt or some feeling of mistake. The war you see is very frightening.

I agree. There's something about those war years – such enchanting movies made in the worst time we'd ever had. I find the tone very troubling sometimes, rapturous but damaged. Have the movies led us astray? Connected us or cut us apart. I'm not sure. The two children in the book are precious.

When I look at these books as a trilogy, they seem to me as comprehensive as the Biographical Dictionary *and the most revealing or personal work you've done.*

I hope so. They are film commentary, but they're novels too. And that is what I most wanted to do.

Very good. So how are you feeling now?

Pretty good, I think.

Excellent, because the car is waiting patiently. One and two are excited to see you again.

THANK YOU

Is this your author speaking? Can you rely on him? Or am I just writing him?

But I want you to trust my thanks: to Laura Morris for making the arrangement with Oldcastle, and to the several people there who made working on this book, and the new edition of the trilogy, such a pleasure. I mean Ion Mills, Claire Watts, Ellie Lavender, Nick Rennison, Steven Mair and Ifan Bates. I have never known a publishing team so concerned with detail, or so dedicated to the spirit of the enterprise.

I need to mention another friend and inspiration. As I was reading the proofs for *Connecticut*, on February 13 2023, Tom Luddy died in Berkeley, California. In 1985, the first book in the trilogy, Suspects, was dedicated to Tom. It's not that he contributed to the books directly, but he was such a friend and guide on film in America that I think of him as the godfather to these novels. I believe he understood and shared in the mad way characters in movies can become our secret fellows in life.

Ultimately an examination of how movies affect the way we think and how film not only shapes our perceptions and our memories but in some ways comes to stand in for them, *Suspects* is the most inspired of commentaries on film noir and Hollywood story-telling. At once a cinematic tour-de-force and a dazzlingly original work of fiction, the narrator's identity is gradually revealed as the central mystery unfolds.

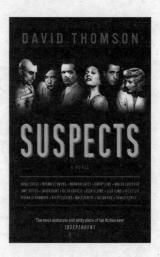

KAMERABOOKS.CO.UK/SUSPECTS

From 1865 to 1950, the multi-faceted world of the American West, its rich, colourful characters, and its many faces – historical, mythic, and cinematic – are captured in the story of a reclusive, elderly photographer and her friend, a writer of Western comic books. Combining history and the fabricated realities of film, *Silver Light* examines the mythic image of the West and its meaning for Americans.

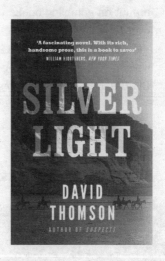

KAMERABOOKS.CO.UK/SILVER-LIGHT

●LDCASTLE BOOKS

POSSIBLY THE UK'S SMALLEST
INDEPENDENT PUBLISHING GROUP

Oldcastle Books is an independent publishing company formed in 1985 dedicated to providing an eclectic range of titles with a nod to the popular culture of the day.

Imprints vary from the award winning crime fiction list, NO EXIT PRESS (now part of Bedford Square Publishers), to lists about the film industry, KAMERA BOOKS & CREATIVE ESSENTIALS. We have dabbled in the classics, with PULP! THE CLASSICS, taken a punt on gambling books with HIGH STAKES, provided in-depth overviews with POCKET ESSENTIALS and covered a wide range in the eponymous OLDCASTLE BOOKS list. Most recently we have welcomed two new sister imprints with THE CRIME & MYSTERY CLUB and VERVE, home to great, original, page-turning fiction.

oldcastlebooks.com

| OLDCASTLE BOOKS | KAMERA BOOKS | HIGHSTAKES PUBLISHIN
| POCKET ESSENTIALS | CREATIVE ESSENTIALS | THE CRIME & MYSTERY CI
| NO EXIT PRESS | PULP! THE CLASSICS | VERVE BOOKS